Julian Rigby and the Keepers of Time

Julian Rigby and the Keepers of Time

For information please contact jsgrammatico@yahoo.com.

Publication by Shelby House
Edited by Julie Gray

First Edition: April, 2012.

Printed in the U.S.A.

ISBN 978-0615620770

Julian Rigby
and the
Keepers of Time

By John S. Grammatico

For my sons, Dominic and Vincent.
(aka Dom Sawyer and Huckleberry Vin)

May you always find adventure together.

ONE

Fight or Flight?

London's Westminster Under School had always annoyed Julian; from the chokehold of its mandatory bowties to its well-manicured maze of shrubbery bearing false welcome to students it would soon herd like cattle.

Even its name begged to be mocked. 'Under School'. Could it have reminded Julian any more of *under*pants? Or *under*arms? How could students take themselves seriously in such a ridiculously named institution?

Oh, but they did. Every last one of them. Generations of young boys had become men in the Westminster Under School. They were part of a legacy.

To prove it, somber quotes loomed over every archway of every classroom door. Quotes like, "*The boy is father to the man*," whatever that was supposed to mean.

It was tosh, all of it. At least, to Julian Rigby it was. The awkward, quirky twelve-year-old boy sat frozen in his chair in the headmaster's office as if he were an insect trapped in a chunk of amber for all time. He stared at a clock on the wall while yet another lecture went in one ear and out the other.

"Fear is a useless emotion, Julian," said the headmaster, a brooding man with one grey hair for every boy he'd ever taken into his custody, "And one that won't serve you well once you've transferred this fall to Westminster Academy for Young...*Men*." The headmaster lingered on that last word, to make sure Julian understood the significance.

But Julian's attention was one hundred and twelve percent given to the nagging, ticking, tocking, clicking, clocking wall clock. He knew it was no ordinary clock.

It was an infinity clock. The outer rim was copper with a smooth, shiny finish. But instead of completing a circle, it made a perpetual spiral, forming several incomplete, concentric circles. Each one was smaller than the last as the spiral got tighter and tighter, and every one had its own sand-colored clock face with its own set of deep brown, liquid-like numbers that warped as if they were being pulled into the center.

Inside of each set of numbers were sets of hands that all ticked in unison.

That ticking felt like torture to Julian, reminding him of the endless ticks and tocks of Granddad's clock shop below their apartment –

and his bedroom. Many a night he considered smashing every one of those clocks just to get a decent night's rest.

To make things worse, the halls outside the headmaster's office were filled with anxious students. Their voices grew louder and more unified as they counted the seconds remaining in this year's school term, "Twenty-Five! Twenty-Four! Twenty-three!"

How slowly the hands on that infinity clock seemed to move, Julian thought. How irritating its ticking and tocking was. He remembered what he'd read of Chinese water torture and imagined it could be no more painful than this.

"Eighteen! Seventeen! Sixteen!" the incessant noise in the hallway continued. Julian shifted his gaze up to the very serious quotation painted over the infinity clock –"*Look back too often and you will soon be headed that way.*"

"At the Academy, you will no longer be able to run from your problems, Julian. You will be expected to face them head on." Headmaster Benson stood in front of the boy, blocking his view of the infinity clock and the curious quote.

"Super. Looking forward to it," the boy mumbled.

"What was that?" asked the headmaster.

"Nothing." Julian's eyes wandered around the room, drifting conveniently past his own reflection in a stained glass window that offered only more of what he did not care to see. Unruly brown hair, oversized front teeth and the awkward way he looked in the Westminster school uniform – or as he called it, the three B's – blazer, bowtie and bum cover.

The headmaster droned on. Unnoticed, Julian arose from his chair and approached a looming bookcase. He spotted a title on the shelf that interested him, and pulled the book for a better look. It was *Peter and Wendy*, by J.M. Barrie. Julian skimmed the pages, settling on an image of Peter Pan flying over a city. He considered for a moment how wonderful it would be to fly like him, to live like him, to escape like him. He even imagined his own face on the image of Pan's body and it inspired a crooked little smile.

One that Headmaster Benson did not appreciate. The book was suddenly snatched from his hands and Julian turned to see *that* look, the same one he had seen so many times before that it made him want to throw up.

Adults all think they know best, he thought.

Headmaster Benson stared down into Julian's big, brown eyes. "Have you heard *anything* I've said, boy?" he boomed.

"Ten! Nine! Eight!" The crowd continued to narrate this historic moment of his graduation.

"You must learn to focus. Young men haven't the luxury of time to waste."

Time. Julian was surrounded by time. Why was everybody always talking about time? Take it from a kid who grew up in his granddad's clock shop. Time was a prison.

Again, Julian avoided Headmaster Benson's eyes. This time he queasily noticed what waited for him on the other side of the front glass door, the very reason for his visit to the office in the first place. A threat that pompously went by the name of Martin Winkleman the Third.

Julian knew all about Martin's illustrious family legacy - and his famous aviating father's accomplishments, too. Oh yes, Julian knew all about Martin Winkleman. Martin made sure of that.

But at this particular moment in time, Julian's heightened senses were tuned to Martin's very specific body language. The squiggly vein that danced madly in his neck. Knuckles that changed colors like mood rings. Eyebrows furrowed so close together they looked like two angry, sun-bleached caterpillars squaring off for a wrestle. In his hand and bearing a large bold red scribble was a paper labeled 'B+'.

When was the last time a Winkleman was branded with that scarlet letter? Julian wondered.

"Four! Three!" nagged the chorus of that most dreadful symphony.

Julian was startled out of his reverie when Headmaster Benson took his hand and said in a soft, sympathetic tone, "I know what you've been through, Julian."

"Two! One!"

"But you must believe that eventually, with time..."

BBRRIINNGGG!

Saved, by every bell in every hallway that rang at the end of an era for the one hundred and one graduating boys of Westminster Under School who poured out the front doors of the institution like sprung prisoners reintroduced to daylight.

But Julian's race to freedom wasn't going to be quite as easy. Because the only exit from *this* office offered a confrontation he wasn't ready to have – with a third generation Winkleman, a young man wrapped so tightly in the school colors of maize and green that Julian couldn't determine if his face was red from anger or simply the circulation being cut off by his bowtie.

Enough nodding and agreeing with the dull headmaster, Julian thought. He had to do something and he had to do it fast.

Quick as lightning, he ducked under the hand of Headmaster Benson, slid on the seat of his short pants along the slick surface of his mahogany desk, and snatched a fresh ruby-red apple along the way.

As he landed in front of three very serious-looking windows on the opposite wall, Julian stopped for a quick bite of the apple. "Sorry, Headmaster Benson, but..." Swiftly, he raised the center pane of one of the tall windows. A white dove perched outside the sill fluttered away and a rush of warm summer air flowed in. He raised himself to the sill and finished his thought with, "...I've got to run."

Julian clicked his heels together once, hard. Suddenly, the soles of his shoes unfolded to the sides and were replaced by wheels. He swung his scrawny legs over the window's edge into the outside world and simply dropped out of view from the second story window.

It all happened so fast that Headmaster Benson didn't even have time to rush after him.

What Julian remembered all in a dizzying rush, that Headmaster Benson may not have, was that the outside surface of that window was not a straight drop of rugged brick and mortar as one might have expected.

No, this happened to be the center column of the building's exterior façade and was covered with a silky smooth decorative concrete that, as it traveled farther down, curved away from the building at such a subtle degree it eventually joined seamlessly with the asphalt of the parking lot below. It was so notable a design that skateboarders came from all over London to ride up and down those columns, performing tricks.

Tricks I have no idea how to do, thought Julian, as he soared down the concrete ramp from nearly twenty feet high. With the ground rapidly approaching, Julian made a quick calculation and realized that, as a matter of physics, he may be in over his head.

The drop from that window plunged Julian down the side of the wall faster than he anticipated. By the time his wheels met with the asphalt of the parking lot, he was screaming blue murder. But who could hear it? The entire campus was crawling with screaming students, excited to begin their summer.

His hair whipping into his eyes, Julian soared across the parking lot and straight into a group of foam-covered students engaged in a celebratory shaving cream fight.

Julian sailed through the shaving cream battleground, precariously bouncing off of students and ricocheting like a pinball until – SPLAT – he went directly through a massive glob of shaving cream that not only filled his mouth and muffled his tender screams, but also covered his eyes!

That might not have been so horrible if his wheels hadn't already gained more speed on the smooth asphalt, thanks to its downward slope toward the street.

The street! Frantically, Julian wiped the shaving cream from his eyes as the sounds of traffic got closer and louder but what was left of his vision was unreliable, at best. By this time he had already felt himself drop down the curb and into the road. A dangerous game with traffic was not exactly what Julian had in mind.

HONK!

Desperately, Julian struggled to navigate his way across a sea of swerving Mercedes, darting Fiats and screeching Jaguars that attacked him from all sides. His ears were rendered nearly as useless as his burning eyes and foam-filled mouth as a cacophony of honking horns filled the air.

Eventually, Julian's brain gave up. It shut down like a blown power grid, locking out sound and vision entirely and leaving him alone in foamy darkness.

If there was one thing that Julian hated, it was darkness. Ever since he could remember, he had an absolutely paralyzing fear of the dark. His granddad would buy nightlight bulbs in bulk, as Julian could not stomach even a moment without some little shimmer of light.

And in those nights when he did finally fall asleep, Julian would be tormented with the same nightmare - always stuck in a world dipped in black. Always holding a torch about to lose its flame. Always on the losing end of a battle against time.

For years, Granddad had told Julian that it was just a phase. All boys have their phobias and fears and that eventually, with time, Julian would grow out of it.

By now, Julian's roller-wheeling mayhem had drawn the attention of the entire school. All screaming, running, and shaving cream fights had stopped. Everyone watched, fascinated and horrified, as the boy no one understood faced an almost certain demise.

Just before Julian reached the safety of the sidewalk on the opposite side of the street, mere inches before the curb near a public bus stop – his vision slowly began to return and something most peculiar took shape before him.

At first, it appeared to be one of the famous London black taxis that silly tourists so adore. But something about it was different, sinister even. Its body was pieced together with various scraps of metal. The windows were so dark they reflected like mirrors, and smoke bellowed from its front grill like the snort of a charging bull. But strangest of all, there were no wheels. The car appeared to hover over the street.

Perhaps his eyes were playing tricks on him, Julian thought. *After all, who knows what chemicals are in shaving cream and what they are capable of?* There was one thing Julian was sure of, however. If he didn't get out of its way, he'd soon be the hood ornament on that beastly craft.

Like a skinny little rugby player desperate to avoid a tackler in a dive for the line, Julian threw himself head first toward the sidewalk, barely avoiding the raging mystery machine which snagged the fabric of his flowing blazer and tore away a chunk as its souvenir.

RRRIP!

He rolled onto the safety of the patchy, brown grass, still at top speed until finally barreling into a thirteen-year-old schoolgirl like a bowling ball. Her folder burst open, exploding papers everywhere like fireworks.

As the last bits of stinging foam cleared from his eyes and all things blurry sharpened back into focus, Julian peered through the fluttering white papers that fell like giant snowflakes crashing a summer day, to catch his first look at her...the girl with almond eyes.

She was unlike any girl he had ever seen. She had glossy black hair, as straight as an arrow, pulled back into a ponytail so tight it looked like it hurt. Her skin was somewhere between tan and bronze, and her eyes, as he had already noticed, were shaped like almonds.

What he did *not* seem to notice, however, was her rigid body language suggesting that she was not nearly as fascinated by him as he was by her. Julian raised Headmaster Benson's apple, now crushed and covered with shaving cream and chunks of grass and dirt. "Apple?" he offered.

The girl's almond eyes narrowed with the same disdain he had registered earlier in the face of...

"Hello there, Rigby." Martin Winkleman the Third appeared yet again, standing over Julian with a mocking grin.

TWO

One Strange Stroll

A falling piece of paper landed on Julian's head. He pulled it off and turned toward a looming Martin Winkleman.

Julian covered his fear with a nervous smile. "Third, so nice to see you. Looking very... Winkleman-like today." Julian hopped to his feet and began a slow backward glide on his roller shoes.

"Stop saying that. And stop calling me Third." Martin vainly tried to tuck his shirt back into his trousers.

"Bad day for everyone," said Julian as he rolled back farther, picking up a few of the girl's fallen homework papers strewn about the grass. "I say we all just forget it and go home."

Starting to blush, Martin stepped closer. "You know I can't bring *this* home," he gestured to the paper in his hand, marked with the big, red B+.

Suddenly it dawned on Julian. He stopped picking up papers. "You're afraid of what your parents will say!"

Martin tried his best to keep his blueblood composure, "Of course not. But this should have been an A, Rigby, and you know it."

"What a disappointment. Too bad you copied from me. Can't let down your rich parents again, can you?"

Martin's face reddened more. "Stop talking about my parents! I don't care what they think!" Martin was gaining on Julian and, by the looks of his fist, ready to punch him squarely in the stomach.

Soon the two were circling the confused girl with the almond eyes, like hands on a clock gone crazy. "I've never hit anyone who didn't have it coming, Rigby." Martin cocked his fist and took a swing, but Julian ducked it and skated backward.

"Would you two stop it and tell me what's going on?" the girl said, now completely annoyed.

"I've been so rude, Third. Or shall I call you...Sir Martin of the Winkleman Clan?"

"Don't push me, Julian."

"Of course. Let me introduce you to my new friend..." Julian interrupted, motioning to the girl with almond eyes a bit desperately.

She gruffly finished Julian's sentence…"Lily."

Julian thought for a beat and nodded. "Interesting. Don't think I ever met a Lily."

"Don't think you ever met a girl," quipped Martin, as he tracked Julian like prey.

And that was when it happened – Julian's roller shoes hit a pebble and he went flying, landing squarely on his back. He stared up at the sky for a moment to catch his breath, humiliated.

Normally quick with a comeback, he didn't have one for Martin's comment. Because Martin was right. Julian couldn't think of the last time he had spoken to a girl. Then again, he couldn't really think of the last time he'd spoken to anyone, outside of his granddad and the headmaster.

Suddenly, Julian was being raised back to his feet roughly by the lapels of his blazer. Martin looked at him almost apologetically before cocking back his fist again. "This is so it doesn't happen again, Rigby," and as he prepared to serve up his best knuckle sandwich, what happened next was probably Julian's biggest surprise of the day.

With catlike reflexes, Lily deflected Martin's blow with the side of her palm, twisted Martin's wrist behind his back and used his own momentum to hammer his face into the back of the fiberglass bus shelter, cracking the bridge of his nose.

"Ahh!" he screamed, as a thin stream of blood trickled out.

Meanwhile, Lily watched with great disappointment as her school bus drove off without her.

Martin hopped around in pain, pinching his nose and doing his best to remain a gentleman.

Julian stared at Lily with newfound respect. "Well, now, Lady Lily. Have I mentioned that it's been a pleasure to meet you?" he offered with an outstretched hand that she completely ignored. "Do you attend the Country Day School for Girls?" Julian persisted.

Lily looked down at her Country Day homework folder, her Country Day purple skirt and matching blouse, up at the Country Day marquee behind him then back at Julian with her best *duh* face.

Julian laughed off his silly question. "Well, just so you know – what you have witnessed here is merely the mild-mannered alter-ego I use by day. At night, under the cloak of darkness, my true superhero identity reveals itself."

A laugh blurted out from the wounded Winkleman. "You? A superhero? You can't even save yourself." Martin's voice had a newly nasal sound.

Lily tucked her papers back into her folder and took a deep breath. For the first time, she seemed flustered. "Now what am I going to do? Because of you two idiots, I've missed my bus!"

"Can't you just walk?" Julian asked quizzically.

Lily hung her head, then glared up at him. "No, Julian."

"But why, it's no big deal—"

"For your information, my parents won't let me walk home alone."

Julian suppressed a laugh. "They won't? I walk all over London anytime I want." Julian was exaggerating slightly but he had his dignity to regain after landing flat on his back. He spotted some stray grass and swatted it off his shoulder. "It's ridiculous, if you ask me."

"Thanks for the update, Julian." Lily's eyes flashed anger and embarrassment. She looked down at her feet. "My mom isn't from here, okay? She was raised differently and—"

"And you have to be the same way?" Julian interrupted.

Lily's cheeks flamed bright red.

Martin touched his swelling nose tenderly. "Fine, I'll walk you home. If you promise to keep your hands to yourself."

Lily gave Julian a reproachful look as Martin picked up his jacket and his paper. Hesitantly, Martin joined Lily and they began the long trek over Page Street toward the Thames.

Julian retracted the wheels on his roller shoes and watched them go. Winkleman had won again. Sighing, he opened his backpack and took off his blazer.

Maybe not this time.

"So what kind of name is Lily, anyway?" Martin asked.

"A girl's name."

"What I mean is..."

Lily pivoted in front of Martin and poked at his still-throbbing nose. "If you're asking me why my hair is black, my skin darker than yours and why my clothes smell of curry then the answer is that Mother is from India, Bengal to be specific. Is that okay with you or are things going to once again turn physical?"

"Are you two at it again?"

Martin turned to see that Julian had decided to join them on their journey.

Lily glared at him like no girl Martin or Julian had ever seen before.

"I was just trying to make small talk," muttered Martin. He glanced at Julian, embarrassed at his gaffe.

"No such thing as small talk, Winkleman. Only small talkers."

Martin took a look at Julian's exposed T-shirt, airbrushed with muscles to appear like his own. Martin rolled his eyes and brought up the rear.

It was now Julian's turn to speak with Lily. He matched her stride and gave it a try as a growing crowd of excited tourists on their way back from Westminster Abbey clogged his path. "So, what was that back there, Kung Fu? Tae Kwon Do? Ninjitsu?" Julian thought it was time to drive his point home and really impress Lily now that he had her attention. He did some chops, kicks and blocks until one awkward spin took him right into two very annoyed old ladies.

Lily brushed him off with, "Just Karate."

"Cool. You must love it."

"I hate it."

"Cool." He was even more awkward in conversation than Martin, and became more flustered by the moment as the unusually hot sun beat on him and the crowd of tourists grew on the walkway. One of them, in a rush to get in line for roasted nuts from a vendor on the bridge, slammed shoulders with Julian. It was so painful he wanted to cry.

"What's cool?" Lily asked, easily annoyed by Julian. "I tell you that I hate Karate and you say that's cool?"

Julian stammered, "Uh, no. That's not cool at all. It's uncool. Er, wait. I dunno." He realized he was getting nowhere fast – and Martin realized it too, passing him with a smirk.

Lily turned left into an alley loud with barking dogs and ripe with the aromas of Asian cooking. The bright sun didn't reach this place and it was somehow strange and scary, Julian thought. Like a different world. Julian looked at Lily sidelong. "Are you sure this is the way?"

Lily smiled. "Why, are you scared?"

Julian puffed out his chest. Of course he wasn't scared. But this shortcut down an alley was like no place he'd ever been, with its smells of exotic food, and laundry hanging from balconies. "No," Julian lied.

"Don't have much of a sense of adventure, for a superhero," Lily laughed.

Julian laughed along with her, even louder to be sure both she and Martin understood that he was not bothered by her words. "Oh, I'm plenty adventurous alright. Did you not see me playing in traffic back there at the school? It's a hobby of mine. Car dodging. My friends call me Mister Danger...Man...Guy."

For the first time, Lily got a solid look at Julian's silly muscle-painted T-shirt, then up at the skinny neck and childish face popping out of it. "Danger...Man...Guy?"

"Hardly," Martin laughed and wiped a little more blood from his nose. Lily laughed along with him, unaware of Julian's flaming red face and injured pride.

Julian snipped, "I'm sure your life is pretty exciting and filled with adventure, Winkleman. Stub your toe at the opera much with mummy and daddy?"

The three emerged from the alley back onto a busy London street. Martin stopped and stared at Julian angrily. Julian had touched a nerve and he knew it. "You think you're so smart with your wise cracks and gadgets," Martin delivered, "But you're just an orphan with a bunch of free time and no one to spend it with." A look of faint shame passed over Martin's face. He'd gone too far and he knew it.

Julian was left once again without any wisecrack in his arsenal. Only complete emptiness. He sat down on the curb. "You guys go on. I have to go..." he gestured weakly, "That way. Left. Or right."

A few feet ahead Lily stared daggers at Martin, who shuffled his feet awkwardly. She elbowed him sharply. "Ah-hem."

Making his way through the crowd, Martin reluctantly approached Julian, "I – I'm sorry for that, Rigby. I didn't mean it." He looked back at Lily for approval. She gave none. "And I've decided that your beating can wait until the next time I see you. Call it a rain check, of sorts."

Julian looked up from his feet and forced a smile, "Technically, you're supposed to write it down on a piece of paper to make it official. Something like, 'I.O.U. one punch in the face'."

They both held in a chuckle that wanted to come out. "But I'm not going to apologize for what you started. Got it?" Martin insisted.

Julian nodded, acknowledging that it was the best offer he'd get.

Lily seemed pleased that the two had forged a temporary peace treaty in the best way they knew how. "We'll need something to drink or I'll be dead of dehydration soon," she added to swiftly change the subject.

"My granddad's clock shop is just down that way. We have plenty to drink in the kitchen there," Julian offered. Despite the rough road they had just traveled, Julian didn't want them to part ways quite yet. It was the first time he'd had people to talk to outside of school who were actually his own age.

Lily squinted to find the shop he pointed to in the distance. "Ah, you mean the one with that strange-looking machine out front?"

"Machine?" Julian puzzled. "There's no strange-looking machine out front of the Emporium."

"Okay, then what do you call something that's shaped like a black taxi except twice as large?"

Julian's heart sank. *Did she say Black Taxi?*

THREE

The AM/PM Emporium

In a cramped, quaint clock shop, on a dusty wooden shelf, sat a meticulously handcrafted miniature replica of the most famous clock in England, Big Ben.

An old, meaty hand steadily lifted the not-so-Big Ben with great care and, with a feather duster, wiped the shelf beneath it before setting it gently back in place. "There you are, love," said a tender voice that blended in with the soothing ticking tocking and clucking clocking that filled the shop.

The hand, the voice and the clock shop itself all belonged to Freemont Rigby, Julian's proud guardian and grandfather. With his bushy mop of white hair and kind hazel eyes, he couldn't have been better suited for the job.

The details of the tiny Big Ben were remarkable, carved from white walnut with limitless patience. From the ornate peaks of its gothic arches down to the symmetry of its working hour and minute hands, Freemont's passion for the artistry of clocks and the passing of time was obvious. There wasn't a famous clock that existed anywhere in the world that old Freemont hadn't already carved, sculpted, whittled or otherwise shaped into a delightful miniature.

He continued to wind the rest of his little friends, from the charming wooden cuckoos to the mesmerizing infinity clocks like the one at Westminster Under School. Even the large, disc-shaped clock that wasn't for sale, but proudly bore the Rigby Coat-of-Arms.

Freemont loved every clock almost as much as he loved Julian.

Freemont chuckled to himself; he knew that the sound of all these clocks ticking at once was maddening to some people, especially Julian. But for him, it was soothing. It felt like they were serenading him in their own way. Julian might come to love the sound as much as he did, one day, if the future held what he hoped for.

The old man frowned slightly then straightened his warm, thick sweater and lifted his favorite tea mug – the one with the words 'World's Greatest Granddad' finger-painted on it long ago. He smiled and toasted, "To Julian. World's greatest grandson."

Freemont took a sip of sugary tea from his mug. Julian. His hope for the future. He stared into the bottom of the cup and smiled softly. *Everyone has a secret*, Freemont thought. *This cup is mine.*

Freemont's thoughts were interrupted by a noise outside the window. A beautiful white dove was fluttering its wings strangely up against it as if trying to tell him something. He chuckled. "Good day to you too, mate."

Eventually, the bird fluttered away, but Freemont continued to stare out the window. He frowned for the second time that day. Julian was late coming home from school.

Before Freemont could think more about Julian's whereabouts, he heard the bell on the shop's door tinkle, followed by a different sound.

Thump, drag. Thump, drag.

Freemont had a visitor, and a visitor with quite a limp, by the sound of it. *I know just how you feel, mate,* Freemont thought, as he picked up his trusty cane.

Slowly, Freemont made his way through the aisles of clocks toward the front counter. *Should get some of those roller contraptions, like Julian has,* he joked to himself. He called out a rhyme that he'd greeted so many others with before, "Welcome to the AM/PM Emp-or-eee'-um. My own personal time mus-eee'-um. If it's a clock you seek, look around and see 'um. Or tell me your wish and I'll make it be 'um."

Usually this is where customers would clap or chuckle or attempt to rhyme in return. But this time, on this day...there was no reply. Only that unusual sound again.

Thump, drag. Thump, drag.

Freemont arrived at the front of his shop to find a stranger who stood lean and tall with his back turned. The man was clad from head to toe in what looked like a black, leather flight suit woven with medieval fabrics.

A glint on his right boot buckle drew Freemont's eye. As did a leather strap that wrapped around the boot several times, then up his leg and around his waist.

Freemont swallowed the growing uneasy feeling he had inside and forced a smile. He watched as the stranger tilted his head up to read the sign over the door: *Time and Tide Wait for No Man.*

The stranger scoffed at it, then slowly pulled the drawstring on the front window blinds, shutting out the harsh sunlight.

Freemont forced a nervous laugh, "Yes, sorry 'bout that. Some strange sunny weather we're having today. Almost not sure we're in London any more."

The dark stranger untied another thin black leather strap from the back of his head, removing a dusty pair of thick-rimmed goggles from his long, greasy black hair, then set them on Freemont's front display table.

Freemont felt compelled to remove the dirty goggles immediately, for that table held so many of his very best showpieces. His precious little 'children'.

The stranger's boots resumed their noisy rhythm as he calmly browsed the merchandise on that table.

Thump, drag. Thump, drag.

He passed a six-foot tall sand-filled hourglass. He examined its mechanical frame that resembled a chiropractor's inversion table allowing it to be easily turned on its head.

"That's my 24-Hour Glass," Freemont offered proudly. "It's perfectly calibrated down to the last grain."

The stranger did not respond.

Thump, drag.

Next, he passed a miniature replica of an ancient sundial, dragging the palm of his fingerless leather glove across its surface, making Freemont ever more uneasy.

"I do ask that you not touch the merchandise, sir."

The stranger then turned his attention to an extremely delicate glass miniature of a grandfather clock with three glass hearts as pendulum weights. Freemont tagged only this piece and the Rigby Coat-of-Arms clock with labels that read 'Not For Sale'.

The dark stranger lifted it high, looking past his own grimy fingernails to examine its remarkable craftsmanship.

Freemont stepped behind the counter, gripping his cane. It was perhaps the most ornate and beautifully-engraved sculpture in the entire shop. His thumb nervously caressed the three doves that were carved into its golden handle. *More artifact than antique*, he would tease Julian about the cane. *Of the two of us, one is older than time itself.*

Freemont gently pointed his trusty cane at his guest and said, "Careful with that piece, mate. It's a one-of-a—"

SMASH!

The dark stranger threw the tiny clock violently to the floor. Glass skittered across the floor and scattered into every corner, crevice and crack it could find.

Freemont stared in shocked silence.

"Oh, I think it is *you* who should be more careful, old man," the visitor scowled.

Freemont took a wobbly step back, terror mounting as he began to recognize the stranger.

The stranger turned from the shadows to reveal his pale, stubbly face and soul-piercing white-colored eyes.

Freemont's heart skipped a hundred beats. His own face turned as white as his hair. His knees buckled, and his stout frame dropped onto the stool beneath him.

Thump, drag.

The stranger stepped closer to examine Freemont's face. He studied it as if only he was able to read the stories hidden in each wrinkle.

A single word fell from Freemont's mouth as if it had been hidden in there for years and only now jostled free. "Gabriel." *It is him,* Freemont thought. He felt it in his bones. And suddenly a sickening feeling he hadn't felt in his gut in many moons returned.

Everything about Gabriel made Freemont ill, even the way he savored the taste of his own dirty name in the air.

"It's been a long time since I heard it out loud, old friend," Gabriel said through his clenched, yellow-stained teeth.

Freemont secretly reached his trembling right hand under the counter and silently flipped a white switch.

With all the courage and calm he could muster, Freemont pushed off his antique cane, and rose fully to his feet. The color slowly returned to his cheeks as he lifted his chin high and proud. "I am not your friend, Gabriel. And that was your doing. Not mine."

Gabriel responded with a dismissive roll of the eyes. "*That* I did not miss. Your pageantry and pride," he sighed.

Freemont began to respond, "You were equally not missed—"

But he was swiftly interrupted. "Would you believe that despite not speaking for, what has it been, twelve years, I am already bored with this conversation?" Gabriel unbuckled one of the many iron clasps on his ragged flight suit and jerked on a strap that unraveled around his body like an obedient serpent, falling to the floor in a coil of leather. He held the other end of the strap like a bullwhip.

WHHHHHSTT!

With a flick of his wrist, he sent the leather slithering around Freemont's cane. A quick tug, and the cane was yanked away from Freemont, forcing him to crash into the front display table, exploding several more glass clocks like fireworks.

CRASH! CRASH! SHATTER!

Freemont stumbled to the wooden floor, the palms of his old, meaty hands barely catching his fall.

A dirty boot stepped on his fingers. Freemont wanted to scream in agony, but refused to give Gabriel the pleasure.

Along the hardwood floor plank, he took solace in the beautifully carved handle of his cane, the golden doves that suddenly made him think of the one that had fluttered outside his window. *Was it warning me of Gabriel?* he wondered.

"What say we skip the stroll down memory lane and you just give me what I want?" Gabriel whispered into Freemont's ear, his breath rank and hot.

Freemont felt his chest pound louder and louder by the second. He wasn't able to control his blood pressure though he desperately tried. "My heart, Gabriel, is weak. I am not the man I was years ago when...*it* happened."

Gabriel released the old man's hand from his boot, but only to step back with laughter. "It?" He scoffed and ran a filthy finger over a glass cabinet full of Freemont's tiny masterpieces. "It? Such an insignificant little word..." Gabriel gently tipped one of Freemont's clocks toward the edge of the shelf, "...For such a grand event, don't you think?"

SMASH!

A pint-sized replica of St. Mark's Clock in Venice, gone.

SMASH!

A lovely homage to the original lamppost clock in New York's Grand Central Station, destroyed. "No, Monty. I much prefer the name you and your men have given it in your history books. The Second Great Battle, is that it? Yes, that is much more worthy."

Freemont's eyes widened. *How did he know we called it that? He's toying with me*, he thought.

"Forgive me, though," Gabriel continued, "As I tend to profess the only true *greatness* displayed in that battle was by yours truly. I know. I know. Your people see it another way. Let us just agree to disagree on that, for now. It's much more civil, wouldn't you say?"

SHATTER!

The beautifully detailed white walnut replica of Big Ben, ruined.

Freemont's eyes widened with worry. This was going dangerously too far. And Julian might be home any minute.

"That's right, Freemont. I've been catching up with old friends all day. And I hope, for your sake, that our reunion goes better for you than it did for your mates."

Freemont's heart filled with the rage of ten men. If Gabriel had gotten to the Keepers... With great effort, he reached for his cane.

Gabriel stepped on his hand again. He leaned down, very close to Freemont's ear. "Let us cut to the chase..." Gabriel hissed. "Tell me the location of the Sacred Object."

Slowly, Freemont pushed himself up from one knee, and then with Herculean effort, to his feet. The muscles in his jaw hardened and his now-bulging, hazel eyes glared into the milky pupils of his nemesis as he delivered with great clarity and conviction his truest and most noble words. "I am the only one who knows where the Sacred Object lies, and I will die before I ever tell you."

Suddenly, the clocks in the shop were drowned out by the sounds of sirens and screeching tires outside.

Gabriel leaned over the counter and noticed the white silent alarm switch. The corner of his stubbly mouth turned up with a dirty, little grin as he replied, "That can most certainly be arranged."

FOUR

The Bridge Club

The back door of the clock shop burst open and Julian rushed in. Something was wrong. He just knew it. Cautiously, he made his way to the front of the shop. Broken glass was everywhere.

"Granddad?" Julian spun around, searching and surveying the damage. He was confused, not only by the mess, but also, by the many oddities that leapt out at him.

Granddad's stool was spinning, but it impossibly appeared to go both clockwise and counterclockwise at the same time.

Within a single shaft of sunlight from the front window, dust was floating up, not downward, highlighting Granddad's cane on the floor.

And perhaps the strangest thing Julian noticed was that, for the first time in his entire life, the clock shop was...SILENT. Even the clocks left unharmed were not ticking. It was as if they refused to. As if time, for them, had stopped.

Suddenly, Julian's concentration was broken by the sound of police officers kicking open the front door. One dropped low, another stayed high, and two more rushed in from the back. Julian could tell from the looks on their faces that they believed they had caught a vandal red-handed.

"Freeze!"

"To your knees!"

"Hands up!"

Commands were shouted at him from all directions. Julian knew he wouldn't have the chance to explain. He fell to his knees, hands clasped behind his head.

The policemen closed in on him like a pack of hungry wolves.

The shaft of light on Granddad's cane dissipated, sending it back into the shadows where it stayed hidden.

Suddenly, as a bobby handcuffed Julian, the clocks all came alive again, ticking and tocking in a deafening roar, as if they were trying to shout something.

CUCKOO CUCKOO DING DONG CUCKOO!

The cacophony was overwhelming. Julian's eyes darted frantically outside, searching for a friendly face.

He hoped to catch a glimpse of the closest thing he had to friends: a tomboy he hardly knew and a third-generation aristocrat, but they weren't there.

Where is Granddad? What happened to the shop?

Faintly, as if from a great distance, he heard the police sharing snide remarks as they sifted carelessly through the damage.

"Vandalism is an act of immaturity," said one.

"Maybe if we start treatin' these lads as adults it'll force 'em to grow up," replied another.

"Well said," chimed a fat policeman with a very red face. "It's time boys like this got a taste of life...*on the other side.*"

"Where is my granddad? What happened here?" Julian shouted.

"Likely story," laughed one of the policemen. He affected a younger sounding voice as he mimicked Julian, " 'Where's my granddad?' " He laughed. "Nice try. Bring him in."

And just like that, Julian found himself in the back of a paddy wagon, being driven to the nick.

It seemed like days, but it was only hours before darkness gave way to light as a lumbering, steel door slid open with a screech. Harsh, fluorescent light flooded Julian's holding cell. Immediately, he pushed himself up and away from the corner he had curled into and rose to face a beefy man no taller than he, with a shiny bald head and piercing, dark eyes. He looked oddly like a—

"Julian Rigby?" the fire hydrant spouted.

"He's on holiday for the week. Did you want to send him a post?" Julian was trying his best to cover his fear, his worry and his frustration. He had to get out of this jail, and fast. Darkness was his sworn enemy and claustrophobia went hand-in-hand with the dark.

The man was not amused. "I am CAP Detective Riley," the fire hydrant said emotionlessly.

Julian tried to appear confident as he dusted off his pants, straightened his shirt and hair and, with a quick pass of a sleeve, made quite sure there were no moist remnants of tears under his eyes. "CAP Detective? You look for clues to determine the whereabouts of lost hats?"

"CAP is an acronym for my unit. Crimes Against Persons." The man looked at Julian as if he were an idiot.

"Well, in that case – I have a long list of grievances to file with your unit about certain crimes against this person right here. Starting with the broken light bulb in this God-forsaken cell!" Julian never fancied himself much of a shouter, but then again he was never much for sitting alone in the dark for three hours, either.

He once read that a fear of the dark is not fear of darkness itself, but rather a fear of what is concealed within the dark, coiled and waiting.

There was something about Julian that only Julian and Granddad knew: every night Julian found himself lost in the same nightmare. It was a world dipped in black in which Julian held a torch about to lose its flame. Terrible things happened in his dreams. Julian drowned or fell or burned up. And it was always oppressively dark.

Getting rid of these bad dreams was something Julian was working, with none too much success. He knew this fear had something to do with his parents' death, but he never dared ask Granddad. Granddad never seemed ready to talk on it. He only ever said that it had happened when Julian was a baby, that his parents loved him deeply, and that, sadly, they were gone. Forever.

"Listen here, lad," offered the Detective. "I'm not big on apologies, but you're right about the light bulb."

Julian pasted on his best adult face. "It will all be in my letter to your superiors."

"Are you okay, then? My officers told me they heard...whimpers."

All composure Julian had was suddenly thrown out the window, "Whimpers? Try grunting, sir! That was grunting. For your information, I was doing push-ups to stay fit in the event that I need to lead a prison riot."

The detective stared at Julian wryly. "That right?"

"Yes. And in the course of doing push-ups, one thousand to be specific, I tend to grunt. I also grunt when running marathons, hiking mountains and slaying large beasts, if you must know. Now with whom do I speak about getting my one phone call and perhaps a jailhouse tattoo?"

Detective Riley calmly stepped out of Julian's way and motioned for him to walk freely out the cell door. "No need for either of those, lad. You're being released. Just a misunderstanding. Our officers were only doing their job."

"Well, I intend to discuss this at length with my solicitor," Julian said with aplomb.

“Do you now?” The detective smiled at Julian patiently.

As they walked together down a narrow corridor of Westminster Station #5, Julian ignored the fact that he was not at all in the vast prison he had imagined, packed with hardened criminals.

No, this was more like a dentist’s office with brick walls instead of plaster ones.

Suddenly, Julian stopped walking. “Wait, you said you were from Crimes Against Persons?”

Detective Riley kept walking without him, “Yes.”

“I didn’t know you folks handled vandalism cases.”

The detective stopped and, without turning around, answered, “We’re not sure this is a vandalism case anymore. Can’t say this early, but it might be a Missing Persons.”

Though Julian knew in his sinking heart what the man meant, he couldn’t help but reply. “But I’m right here, Detective. Riddle solved. Tea and scones for everyone.”

The detective then turned and looked at the boy with a face that spoke a thousand words – lucky for the detective, since he didn’t seem to want to speak those words himself. He handed

Julian a business card. "Call me if you hear word from your granddad. Or, for anything." Without a backward glance, the detective continued to walk down the hall of the station toward the front office.

"Wait a minute," shouted Julian down the long corridor. "If Granddad's not here, then who am I to be released to?"

Just then a blur of white fur leapt from nowhere and clamped its little jaws on the detective's business card, stealing it from Julian.

"Petey?" said Julian, more pleased than surprised. Petey was a familiar little creature, indeed. The only albino ferret he'd ever seen. And he belonged to Granddad's friend from the Bridge Club.

"Petey, come!" said a voice he expected to hear.

Julian rounded the corner near the front office and there they were, the Bridge Club.

"Julian." The pet's owner, Bishop, nodded sternly as he put Petey back on his shoulder. He was the one with the closely cropped brown beard. Granddad called him "the scientist". A 65-year-old no-nonsense chap dressed crisply in a pressed white shirt with thin blue pinstripes, grey vest and a wide paisley necktie that hung only to the top of his belly.

"Bishop." Julian nodded back, equally as stern. It was a serious situation, after all. Julian had never quite understood Bishop. He knew he came from a military family so in some ways he understood why he was so rigid. But, Julian often thought he might do better with people if he treated them half as well as he did Petey.

The man next to Bishop stood up from his chair and gently addressed the boy. "Evening, Julian." This was Sir Alfred. His long, wispy grey beard, combined with his tweed blazer and wire-rimmed glasses, gave him the look of an aged professor. Either that, or a well-dressed wolf man. Julian still hadn't decided which was a more accurate description.

These men of Granddad's Bridge Club were like uncles to Julian, though not as friendly as real uncles might be. Real uncles, Julian assumed, bring you birthday presents and play with you when they visit. But these chaps were more like fixtures in the scenes of his life, background characters in the photos of his memories.

On most evenings, they would sit at the card table in the back kitchen of the clock shop, drinking ale and having a puff on their pipes. He would often hear the sounds of their voices but never actual words. It was as if they were intentionally speaking extra low so that he couldn't make it out. Which was fine by Julian, as they couldn't possibly have been talking about anything interesting.

Sir Alfred signed a piece of paper on a clipboard held by Detective Riley, then turned to the boy. "We'd like for you to join us, Julian. We have something to discuss."

"You're free to go, lad," the detective added.

As the three of them headed out the station door, Julian looked around. "Where's Linus?"

Just then, Sir Alfred's shoe stepped in a ferret dropping and slid against the slick tile. "Ugh, Bishop. I grow more tired of your furry little creature by the day. And his incessant need to mark everywhere we go with...*pellets*."

Bishop tucked Petey inside his vest protectively. He snarled, "My *creature* has a name. Maybe if you called him by it, he'd stop relieving himself around you." Then he turned to Julian and said, "All great men have great pets, Julian. Remember that."

As the three stepped out of the station and into the cool London nighttime air, Julian looked again for Linus.

Linus was the final member of Granddad's quartet. *After all,* Julian thought, *you can't have a game of bridge with just three players.*

Bishop and Sir Alfred continued walking with no mention of the missing member of the group.

"Petey thinks we should go this way. It's quicker." Bishop pointed toward the left.

"Does he speak to you, Bishop?" Julian asked.

"Don't encourage him, Julian," added Sir Alfred as the three shuffled down the steps and into the humid tube station.

That train ride was one of the strangest of Julian's life. He couldn't seem to stop his whirling thoughts. There he was, in the crowded tube, with two strangely silent old men and with so many questions he didn't know the answers to. Like where Granddad was and what terrible thing had happened earlier today in the old man's beloved clock shop.

Finally, they arrived at their stop and walked briskly to the front door of a very unassuming store.

Julian looked up to read the ragged, old sign, "Chronus Family Cleaners. Are we getting our shirts pressed?" he asked in an attempt at humor that fell on deaf ears. He was now thoroughly confused. *A Dry Cleaner's?*

FIVE

Chronus Family Cleaners

Julian couldn't believe what he was seeing. Hundreds – no – thousands of serpentine clothing racks carried plastic-coated garments, looping around in different directions like an elaborate ballet, never crossing or tangling with one another.

It was dizzying, to say the least. *How could a little store be so…big?* Julian wondered as he looked back to find the front entrance again. But it seemed so far away now.

Even more intriguing, perhaps, was the giant hole in the brick wall to his left. "What happened there? Looks like a truck drove through your wall."

Bishop petted Petey calmly and answered, "Yes, it does. But where are the tracks? Do you see any grooves in the tile from the weight of the vehicle? Any marks from the rubber of the tires?"

Bishop was right, Julian thought. How strange that no physical clues were left behind. Except—

Something caught Julian's eye. It was a small piece of cloth on the ground near the impact site at the wall.

"Look, Julian. I'm not quite sure how to explain the complexity of it all." Sir Alfred watched as Julian ignored him and walked toward the hole in the wall.

Julian picked up the small piece of cloth and stared at it. It couldn't be. But it was. He felt his throat go dry and his stomach fall a hundred stories. The cloth was the torn fabric from his blazer. *The piece ripped away earlier today by the raging Black Taxi.*

Sir Alfred watched the boy carefully and went on. "You see, neither Bishop nor I ever thought we'd be in the position to explain it. If anyone, it would have been your granddad, Freemont, who would one day pass this information to you. Julian? Are you listening?"

Julian looked up at Sir Alfred quizzically. *What the heck is going on?*

Sir Alfred and Bishop peered at Julian intently. Sir Alfred continued. "And to be completely honest, even he swore on the lost souls of his son and daughter-in-law that he would only tell you when you were ready."

Julian looked from Sir Alfred to Bishop and back. Now he knew the truth. These old men had gone batty. Crazy. Out of their minds. Julian nodded calmly. "Yes, go on."

Sir Alfred glanced at Bishop, and then continued, "There are things we are responsible for. Things your granddad is a very necessary part of."

Bishop threw his hands up in the air and blurted out, "We don't have time for this, Sir Alfred!" Bishop marched up to the boy's chair, put his hands on each side and looked deeply and seriously into Julian's puzzled eyes. "We are not really a bridge club, boy. Sir Alfred, Linus, your granddad and I – we are the eldest members of a secret society called The Keepers of Time. A society that dates back thousands of years."

Julian stared back blankly at Bishop. His eyes shifted slowly back to Sir Alfred and then he nodded understandingly. "Okay," Julian responded.

Bishop nodded back and threw an 'I told you so' look at Sir Alfred. "Thank God, the boy understands. Now where's Petey?"

Julian smiled. "And I am the King of England trapped in a boy's body. So if you could please have your little rat bring me my magic potion, I will return to my full-sized man's body and reclaim the throne and have that wall fixed for you right away." Julian laughed and looked from Sir Alfred to Bishop but they just stared back.

Abruptly, Sir Alfred turned and called, "Please, Julian. Come with us." And with that, he disappeared into the whirling, dancing racks of clothing with Bishop close on his heels.

Julian stood and stared.

As the garments circled around again, Sir Alfred's voice echoed out faintly, as if from a great distance, "Trust us, Julian."

"You guys realize that you're likely going senile, right?" Julian just wanted to go home and find Granddad. These two old men were wasting his time. What he should really do, he thought—

Just then Sir Alfred's hand reached out, grabbed Julian by the arm and *phhhht* – he disappeared into the racks of whirling garments.

Julian felt the sensation of falling; plastic garment bags whooshed past him in a dizzying blur. Before he could make sense of any of it, the two old men were guiding him down a rickety, creaking, impossibly steep spiral wooden staircase that seemed to come from nowhere and go on forever and ever.

Wonderful, Julian thought. *My favorite thing. More darkness.* Julian decided to stay quiet until the two old men reached the bottom of the stairs. Best to make an escape plan while they were distracted. Wherever he was now, he could find his way back out. Enough of these crazy old men. He had to find Granddad.

At the bottom of the stairs Bishop ignited a lantern, casting light onto an old-fashioned elevator with an accordion door.

"The Keepers of Time are a very real and very serious organization, Julian," Sir Alfred continued, as the three boarded the elevator. "An organization that is as old as time."

There is that word again, Julian thought. *Time. Why is it that adults always have to be so obsessed with time?*

The elevator slowly dropped through the dirt-walled cavern. Sir Alfred resumed. "What you are about to see is our chamber. It has not been visited by a nonmember in over a thousand years."

Julian scoffed, "A thousand? Geesh, how old are you guys?"

Bishop narrowed his eyes at the boy, seeming to grow more impatient with him by the second. The elevator jerked to a stop, jostling all three of them. Without taking his eyes off of Julian, Bishop reached for the old wheel that controlled the door. "This is where we Keepers hid this morning when Evil was upon us." He paused. "And if you think it's all so funny, then maybe you should think about this...not all of us made it to the chamber." Bishop cranked the wheel to open the accordion door and revealed a room like nothing Julian had ever seen.

Even the multi-million dollar Winkleman-family-sponsored library at Westminster Under School wasn't appointed so artistically.

The sidewalls curved toward each other, meeting at the ceiling's center in a raised point, giving the room the shape of a cardinal's hat. And painted on every centimeter of their surface were angels and cherubs spiraling around Roman numerals and Latin phrases.

Upon the massive wooden beam that ran the length of the ceiling were exquisite carvings: pyramids of Egypt, sundials of ancient Greece, pillars of Stonehenge and heads of Easter Island, hourglasses of all kinds standing among Greek philosophers in flowing robes. And even more.

Julian had never seen anything so beautiful – or so mysterious.

The floors he found equally as dazzling. Short pieces of dark hardwood were interwoven with lighter ones, zigzagging like snakes across a desert, encased by borders of marble so slick he could see his own reflection.

Along the center of the floor an ornately designed rug made of red silk-like cloth and gold tapestry depicted an epic tale that Julian couldn't quite make out.

Ancient oil lamps hung from the beams overhead and shed filtered light through the ornate carvings on them. The soft glow of the lamps illuminated the most marvelous thing of all – books. Thousands upon thousands of books.

Just one shelf alone seemed to hold more than the entire collection in Headmaster Benson's office. There were books of every size, shape and color. Some bound in leather, some wrapped in cloth. And some, Julian could swear, appeared to be scrolls of papyrus as if from before Biblical times.

At the other end of the grand chamber, a subtle red and blue glow emanated from the embers inside a massive fireplace. With a start, Julian noticed that the combined light of the lamps and fireplace embers ominously cast his shadow as that of a man much larger than himself against the bookshelf, a man of great stature.

"Petey!" shouted Bishop, happy to see his little albino friend at the bottom of the bookshelf, making a mess.

This snapped Julian back to himself, but also confused him. "How did your ferret get down here before us?" he asked Bishop.

"Petey can do a great many things that would surprise the likes of you," Bishop said mysteriously.

"And learning to be house-broken isn't one of them. 'Tis a pity," Sir Alfred chimed in.

"I've asked you not to call him that. It's Petey. Petey." Bishop picked up Petey and stroked him affectionately.

Sir Alfred rolled his eyes sharply. "I didn't call him Pity. I said it *was* a pity."

"Regardless, that word upsets him. You know that."

Sir Alfred waved Bishop off and then tenderly approached Julian. "This chamber, our society, it all exists for one purpose: to protect the natural order of time."

"Protect it from what?" Julian asked.

Bishop gave a look to Sir Alfred as if to suggest he'd handle this one. "Sometimes its enemy is merely accidental...the natural evolution into a state of disorder due to completely random events. Chaos, if you will."

Sir Alfred rolled his eyes again. "Bishop. He's not a cosmologist for heaven's sake."

Bishop nodded, "Right, right." He searched for a simpler explanation. "Julian, with infinite dimensions of time all occupying the same space, sometimes there are collisions that occur and we have...*spillage*."

“Spillage?” Julian repeated.

Bishop continued, trying his best to make it sound elementary. “It’s happened several times. The Great Pyramid of Giza was a result of such spillage.”

Julian pondered, “Wait, you’re saying aliens from another dimension spilled into ours and built the pyramids?”

“No. Not aliens. Well, not really. They were bipedal carbon-based life forms like us. Only they were much more advanced and thus their brains were…well, their heads were the size of watermelons. But that’s not the point. The point is that it was the Keepers’ job to contain such ‘spillage’ by returning the visitors from that example to their own dimension and preventing such future integration.”

Julian was truly amused now, nearly laughing aloud at the ridiculousness of Bishop’s science-fiction story. “And how does one do that, Bishop?”

Bishop looked at Julian. “How does a bird fly?”

“It flaps its wings, duh.”

“Right. It merely does what it does. Just like if a Keeper were to snap his finger in the air.”

Julian stared at Bishop. “Okay look, can you guys let me out of here now?”

Bishop looked at Sir Alfred, who nodded. "Go ahead."

Bishop snapped his finger in the air and a silvery ripple magically emanated from his hand and lapped up against Julian as if it were invisible water. The ripple slowly dissipated, leaving Julian wide-eyed.

"What the heck! How did you do that?" Julian cried.

Sir Alfred attempted to calm him. "It's our craft. One that has been developed over time."

"What is this, some kind of hocus pocus?" Julian asked while backing up.

"No, no." Bishop answered. "It's much more scientific than that, boy. We don't conjure anything. We merely use elements that others don't consider to exist. For example, you see me before you, but what you're not choosing to see..."

Bishop reached up as if he were pulling something out of a very tall drawer. Suddenly, the air twisted and warped as Bishop pulled it like a blanket around him. Then in a silvery ripple, he was gone.

"...is the complex fabric of time draped over me." Bishop's voice came from where he had been standing. Where he was still standing. Julian was completely confused.

Sir Alfred looked at Julian and grinned. "There's more in heaven and earth than meets the eye, Julian. The time has come for you to learn."

SIX

The Keepers' Chamber

Julian stood as if rooted to the ground. Bishop had vanished into thin air.

"It is only a craft, Julian," Sir Alfred explained, trying to make Julian more comfortable with the craziness he'd just witnessed.

"Where'd he go?" Julian stared at the spot where Bishop had been standing a moment ago.

"You're just not choosing to see," an invisible Bishop teased.

"Seriously, this isn't funny." Julian reached out attempting to touch Bishop but as he did, Bishop suddenly reappeared, as he unfolded the blanket of air he'd hidden himself with.

Bishop looked at Julian. "We have a few tools at our disposal: our craft, the Sacred Object. These tools exist to help us protect the order of time from all that threatens it."

"And what threatens it now? Not spillage?" Julian played along.

"Evil," Sir Alfred returned. "You see, time is not for man to *control*, only for us to *protect*. We use our tools to shepherd it along, ensuring that clocks run clockwise, that day turns to night and ..."

Bishop sternly finished the thought that Sir Alfred could not, "...And that life becomes death. Think of us as maintenance men in charge of one giant clock for the entire multiverse," Bishop riddled.

"And the main tool in your toolbox is that...Sacred Object thing?" Julian asked.

"Sort of." Bishop lit the remaining sconces along the wall as he walked toward the other side of the chamber near the large fireplace. He seemed calmer now, following Sir Alfred's lead. "The Sacred Object is, in fact, our most important resource in protecting time, Julian. But it shall only be called upon in the most dire of circumstances."

Sir Alfred furthered, "In the right hands, the Sacred Object is peaceful and benign. But in the wrong hands..." he dared not finish his thought.

As they neared the fireplace, Julian saw more clearly that a huge portrait hung above its marble mantle. The frame of the portrait alone must have been priceless: ornate gold carvings of ivy and flowers befitting a king.

The flickering light from the flame sconces and fire embers illuminated the portrait in shadowy light. At first, it was hard for Julian to make out the details, but slowly he was able to see a flowing robe and silvery hair. It was a man with a shadowed face, Julian could see that much, and on his lap a weighty volume bore a vaguely familiar insignia - a horizontal figure-eight.

The man in the portrait, in fact, began to look more and more familiar the closer Julian got.

He turned back to Sir Alfred and Bishop. "So what exactly is this Sacred Object, and where is it?"

"It is not our job to know that," answered Bishop. "Quite the contrary, it is our job *not* to know."

Frustration was beginning to overtake Julian. "Let me get this straight. Your job is to know nothing about an object you are sworn to protect?"

Sir Alfred approached softly, "Only a man who has proven himself to possess the noblest of hearts, the purest of intentions, and the strength and honor of a true leader can be entrusted by the Society to hold that information, Julian. And that man is known as our Senior Keeper."

"Head Janitor, if you will," Bishop added.

Calmly, Sir Alfred continued. "There have been many over the years, but only one at any given time. Only he is privy to the location of the Sacred Object."

Bishop motioned for Julian to have another look at the portrait above the fireplace, revealing the identity of their most precious member.

"Granddad?" Julian couldn't believe it. He studied the eyes and how they hung low with worry just like Granddad's. He traced the wrinkles in the brow, remembering how Freemont once told him that within each fold was a secret story to tell. He wondered which one hid the sorrowful tale of his parents.

Once again, Sir Alfred placed a gentle hand on Julian' s shoulder. "It is our job, as Elders of the Society, to protect our Senior Keeper from any forces of Evil that wish to steal the power of the Sacred Object." He paused for a breath. Sir Alfred seemed reluctant to finish his thought, "But sadly, today we failed."

Sir Alfred glanced across the room where, against the bookshelf wall, a long, narrow lump of blankets were heaped on a table. "Today, Evil learned the whereabouts of our Senior Keeper and, though Freemont is as strong as the strongest we've had for a thousand years, we fear that, away from this chamber and our protection, he is at a great disadvantage. We believe it is only a matter of time before he is broken and our deepest fears are realized."

Julian's head spun like the spinning racks of garments up above. "Broken? What do you mean, broken?"

Sir Alfred struggled to explain. "I mean that your grandfather's strength is about to be tested and that, sooner or later, we must expect he will divulge our secrets."

Julian's eyes widened. "Are you saying that Granddad was taken somewhere to be...questioned?"

"Somewhere. Somewhen," Bishop riddled.

Julian's growing anxiety faded and he scoffed, "Ugh, here we go again with the nonsense."

Bishop stood tall, pivoted on his heels like a soldier and looked sternly at the boy. "When are you going to get it through your thick skull, lad? Your granddad's not coming back. Not without our help. We must find the Sacred Object or all, and I do mean *all*, is lost!"

Sir Alfred nodded in sad recognition of this simple truth.

Julian sat down hard on a marble bench made, it would seem, for just this purpose, to take time out to think.

Sir Alfred went on. "Julian, the Keepers have been in existence for thousands of years. And though we've been tested before, never have we failed to prevent the power of time from falling into the hands of evil. This proves we've been doing things right with the systems we have in place."

Sir Alfred and Bishop shared a knowing look, and then turned toward Julian meaningfully.

Julian's jaw dropped and he stepped back. "Oh no. No, no, no. I am not a system, I'm a kid!" Julian exclaimed. "What could I possibly do?"

"Your grandfather had great faith in you, Julian. We have to trust that and know that you, being Freemont's closest related kin, have the means to help."

"Me. Right," Julian sighed wearily. "I'm the one who is supposed to help you save the world from evil forces that wish to control time. And why do they want this control, again? To skip past the commercials in a football match?"

Bishop glared at Julian – unappreciative of the sarcastic comment. "It's no laughing matter, boy. In the wrong hands, the Sacred Object would have the power to change the outcomes of past wars, determine future leaders, or simply bring back the dead. And that's just for starters."

Sir Alfred put his hand on Julian's arm. "Julian, this is quite serious. The level of evil here is something you cannot imagine." Sir Alfred exhaled heavily and then looked at Bishop. He gave Bishop a nod.

Bishop lifted the blankets from the long table against the back bookshelf wall, exposing the body of a man frozen in a catatonic state.

Julian gasped in horror, "Linus!"

Linus' bushy eyebrows, his crinkly forehead, his paper-thin lips, everything that came together to create the myriad expressions that so defined him to Julian were now as still as stone.

Bishop bit his lip having to look upon him this way. "Linus would have rather died than expose Freemont. But he wasn't given that choice. This Evil has returned with powers we never anticipated, and for every moment we waste trying to convince you to help us, the world ticks closer to danger. And so does your granddad."

Silence, as Sir Alfred and Bishop waited for Julian to respond.

Julian closed his eyes, teetered, and then...

FLOP!

Julian fell like a sack of potatoes. The portrait of Freemont gazed into emptiness.

"I told you he wasn't ready," Bishop mumbled.

"*MayItellyouashhhhhmmmmk?*" Sir Alfred's voice sounded to Julian as if it were echoing down a tunnel, as if he were dreaming.

"Wha–what?" he managed to blubber.

"May I tell you a story?" Sir Alfred repeated, his voice suddenly clear.

Julian looked around, now wide-awake. He was home, in his bed in the apartment over the clock shop. Was it all a dream? With a jerk, he pulled the covers over his face.

"It is the story of the first time I met your mum and dad," Sir Alfred continued.

Slowly, Julian pulled the covers down. Sir Alfred stood before him, a book in his hands. He caressed the book fondly, but did not open it. "I had already been a Keeper for a good part of my life when Freemont told me of his son's wish to be inducted into the Society with his new bride," Sir Alfred recalled.

"I knew *of* him since his birth, but never really knew *him*. None of us did, as your grandfather tried to shield him from our business. But something happened that suddenly made Freemont change his mind then he strongly supported your father and your mother in their desire to join. Freemont never spoke of what had changed his mind. But in that beautiful ceremony on that beautiful autumn day, it was *she* who answered it for us all."

Julian sat up in his bed, now at full attention.

"You see, Julian, as part of an inductee's ceremony, one must place his hand on the Keepers' Bible and announce his motives for wanting to serve our cause." Sir Alfred smiled, lost in his own memory of her. It was clear to Julian that Sir Alfred had greatly respected his mother.

"Evelyn spoke for them both as she pricked her finger on the tip of the second-hand of the clock in our chamber and spilled a drop of her blood with ours into the Keepers' Urn.

"She proclaimed that she had recurring dreams of a boy that she would one day give birth to."

Julian was stunned to hear that his own mother had also had a recurring dream, just like he did.

"She spoke of his dark, curly hair," Sir Alfred added as he looked at Julian's unruly locks, "And his big, brown eyes."

Julian lowered his eyelids, hyperaware that Sir Alfred was examining him.

Sir Alfred continued, "She told how she could feel his gentle soul. His soft, caring touch." Sir Alfred lifted Julian's chin, prompting him to open his eyes. "Julian, your mother described you right down to your funny little front teeth. I don't know how, but she knew you and loved you long before you were ever born."

Julian's heart began to ache in ways he wasn't familiar with.

Sir Alfred continued, "She told all of us Keepers that she had very high hopes for the boy she would one day mother. How he would be a courageous man who would do amazing things for the world." Sir Alfred stopped to swallow a lump in his throat, which gave Julian only more reason to believe him.

"But she also foresaw great obstacles that stood in his way. And Evil, Julian. Unspeakable Evil. That is why she and your father both dedicated their lives to securing the world for your arrival. They wanted to be sure that the Society was as strong as it had ever been in all of thousands of years to prepare for the coming of...The One."

Julian's eyes filled with tears. His lower lip quivered despite every effort he made to stiffen it. He was paralyzed by the longing he felt for his parents, and daunted by the fear of never living up to his mother's grand expectations. "Do you honestly believe that I have the information you need to save Granddad?" he asked Sir Alfred.

Sir Alfred tried to adjust Julian's bed covers, but only made them worse. It was obvious that he had never tucked anyone in. "I believe you have a lot more in you than that, Julian. But what matters most is what *you* believe."

Julian watched as Sir Alfred turned toward the door.

The old man stopped, thought for a moment, and then set his bible down on Julian's nightstand before turning off the lights.

For the first time, Julian got a good look at the front of that book. A beam of moonlight highlighted the same vaguely familiar emblem that he had noticed in Granddad's portrait down in the chamber. Only this time, the emblem was not partially covered by a hand, and not blurry at all. "Sir Alfred, wait!"

Julian realized it was the first time he had addressed Sir Alfred as 'sir'.

Sir Alfred stepped back in, "Yes?"

"The emblem. I recognize it!" Julian cried excitedly.

Sir Alfred looked at the bible and smiled at the boy. "You recognize the book, Julian.

Freemont held it in the portrait of him over the mantle down in the Keepers' Chamber."

Sir Alfred prepared to turn off the lights once again when Julian responded, "Yes, but that's not the only place that I've seen it. It's also carved into the lock on the family heirloom."

Sir Alfred's eyes grew large. "The family *what*?"

SEVEN

The Family Heirloom

Sir Alfred and Julian rushed down the stairs to find Bishop and Petey inspecting the window blinds like gumshoes looking for clues. Julian would have protested, but right now he hadn't the time to waste.

"The cellar! The cellar!" panted Sir Alfred.

Puzzled, Bishop stepped closer to the base of the staircase. "What cellar?" he asked.

Julian stomped forcefully on the very last stair. "It's where Granddad lets me work on my inventions!"

Bishop looked at him quizzically.

With all of his might and weight, Julian pushed down again on the step. The entire staircase then lifted up like the trunk of a car, revealing a second staircase going down...into a cellar!

Julian led the men down, pulling a string to light another bulb every few steps.

Sir Alfred and Bishop hunched over to accommodate the low ceiling. The stairway had not been made for adult-sized people. Julian descended quickly and gestured at the two men to hurry and join him.

The tiny room was a modest square made of fieldstone and mortar. No fine craftsmanship was wasted down here. It was much more functional than anything up above in the Emporium.

For Julian, however, the cellar was the perfect getaway. A place of his own where he could work on his gadgets, with plenty of tools and random clock parts available and all scattered about.

A pile of discarded roller shoes was heaped in a corner. "That's my reject pile," he muttered.

Sir Alfred and Bishop gazed around mystified by the discovery of this little secret room.

Julian pointed proudly to an invention. "That is what I call the Rigby Knuckle. Combination knife/belt buckle. The pointed edges are safely guarded when stored, but after just a twist of the buckle it pops off and becomes a four-bladed knife perfect for cutting, sawing, slicing and even filing!"

He spotted another invention and proudly lifted it, "And this one is my Jack-in-the-Watch.

Oh, and that one in the corner is a prototype for my…"

"Julian, the family heirloom you spoke of?" Sir Alfred reminded him.

"Ah, right. It's under that cloth." Julian pointed to the far wall where a tall object was covered with a bed sheet.

Bishop carefully removed the sheet to reveal a dusty old grandfather clock.

"Voilá, gents. The family heirloom," Julian said proudly before he was suddenly overcome by a dust-induced coughing fit. After he recovered, he pointed to the decorative, golden lock on the door of the clock, bearing the same horizontal figure-eight design as the emblem on Sir Alfred's bible.

Sir Alfred nodded with a smile at Bishop, who was equally pleased about their discovery.

"Do you know this clock?" Julian asked.

"No, well…sort of," Bishop stammered. "I mean, of course we have seen the miniature replica that Freemont kept on the front display table upstairs. The one he tagged, 'Not For Sale'."

"But we never knew that he had actually built a full scale model somewhere."

Sir Alfred turned to Julian. "Has he told you anything about it?"

Julian shook his head. "He only told me never to touch it. Not even to clean it. To be honest, I never thought there was anything special about it."

Bishop chuckled, "Well, you don't look like anything special at first glance, either. Do you, boy?"

Sir Alfred explained. "Freemont told us the meaning behind the miniature replica years ago. The three glass hearts that hung on each of those pendulums represented your heart, your mum's heart, and your dad's – always moving together through time. Always connected. Your grandfather believed that a heart is..."

Julian interrupted, "—Like a clock. And neither should ever be allowed to stop ticking."

Sir Alfred turned to Bishop, "The boy does have information inside him."

Bishop nodded. "More than he knows." He tugged at the door of the clock but it was locked. "We must get it open," he said to himself more than to anyone else.

Julian lifted a hammer from his pile of tools and raised it high. "In case of emergency, break glass," but before he could make another move, Bishop relieved him of the hammer.

"Hey!" Julian glared at Bishop.

Sir Alfred interceded, "Julian, if Bishop and I are right about what is inside this clock, then any sort of sudden disturbance to it could be catastrophic. We must approach with great caution," he turned to Bishop, "and with great patience."

Just then, Petey rushed down the stairs and ran to Bishop's feet. "What do you think, Petey?" he asked, as he stroked his beloved pet.

Petey sniffed and pawed at the grandfather clock. He rushed around it looking at each of its corners. Then, he squatted and produced another Petey pellet, much to the disgust of Sir Alfred.

"Bishop, please." Suddenly, Sir Alfred was distracted. "Wait, Julian. You said that Freemont told you never to touch the family heirloom. Not even to clean it?"

"That's right. So?" Julian said.

Sir Alfred approached the clock and examined it carefully. He extended his hand toward Bishop. "Your necktie, please."

Bishop clutched his tie. "What for?"

"I'd like to do a bit of dusting," Sir Alfred answered.

Bishop removed his wide paisley tie and handed it over to Sir Alfred, who used it like a feather duster on the clock.

Years of dust fell softly like snowfall from the top of the clock, its side and its face until landing gingerly on the stone floor. But still the clock did not reveal the clues he may have expected to find in its wooden finish.

A squeak came from Petey below, near the fallen dust.

"There!" shouted Julian, "On the floor, look."

Bishop, Sir Alfred and Julian watched in fascination as the powder that had collected on the ground began to form a fiery liquid – and it was moving! Strange, burning, snake-like cursive writing began to emerge.

"That's no ordinary dust," Bishop concluded as he watched the words etch themselves into the stone floor. "It's a powdered chemical reacting with something on the floor. And Petey's discovered it."

Sir Alfred would have rolled his eyes at that if they hadn't been glued to the inscription now forming itself.

Cautiously, Julian drew closer and peered at the strange fiery message materializing in the very place he'd sat a thousand times.

Tick tock. Tick tock.
You stand before a timeless clock.
To crack the riddle of its lock,
Look to the Shepherd. Not the flock.
Only he can solve this rhyme,
To find the key as old as time.

Julian stared at the writing, then at the two men, confused.

"You are the shepherd your granddad refers to, Julian," Sir Alfred noted softly.

"I'm not sure, Sir Alfred. That could mean anyone," Bishop warned.

"It could, but it doesn't," Sir Alfred responded. He turned to the boy, "Read it again, Julian. And think hard. Only you can answer the riddle."

Julian did as he was told, except this time a light bulb lit in his mind. *A key as old as time.* "That's it!" Julian took off running up the stairs, shouting back to them as his footsteps thundered from above. "Granddad always said that between him and this, one of them was as old as time."

Julian came rushing back down the stairs, this time holding Granddad's antique cane. "The cane is the key!"

Bishop looked closely at the tip of the cane and held it next to the lock carefully. He lined up the two complementary images and beamed at Sir Alfred and Julian. "Watch this." Slowly, Bishop pivoted the cane and aligned it with the locking mechanism. Gears began to shift inside and, with a sigh, the door popped open.

Bishop rustled Julian's hair as if he were a pet dog. "Nicely done, boy."

Julian promptly pushed Bishop's hand away. "Thanks."

With great care, Sir Alfred pulled open the glass door and gently slid aside the heart-shaped weights on the pendulums to reveal something extraordinary.

Julian could not believe his eyes. It was something like he'd never seen. And it just hovered, unattached to anything.

It was blue, then pink, then blue again. It took no real shape or texture. And it hummed. It was some sort of energy field, he assumed, that pulsed like a heart. Julian found it intoxicatingly beautiful. "What is it?" he asked, mesmerized.

"A rift," answered Sir Alfred.

"A what?"

Bishop elaborated, "A tear...in the space/time continuum."

Julian gasped. He couldn't take his eyes off the – the "Tear in the space/time continuum!" He spoke with a sudden understanding. "So, *that's* the Sacred Object," Julian concluded.

"No," Bishop said curtly.

Julian's trance was broken. He was shocked. "What do you mean, no? How could it not be? Just look at it. It looks very...sacred. I've never seen anything so darned sacred in all my life."

"You have much to learn, Julian," said Sir Alfred, patiently. "This is but a miniscule example of the *power* of the Sacred Object."

Puzzled, Julian was drawn to the energy of the pulsing rift. He held up his hands as if he were feeling the warmth of a fire. A very strange fire, indeed.

Bishop pulled him back by the shoulder and shook his finger. "Careful, lad. Or you may be in for the ride of your life."

Sir Alfred shuffled toward the staircase. "Come with me, Julian. Let us allow Bishop some time to do what he does."

Reluctantly, Julian followed Sir Alfred. But as he took a backward glance, he couldn't help but wonder... *What does Bishop do, exactly?*

EIGHT

Tea for Two

Upstairs in the tiny kitchenette at the back of the clock shop, where the Bridge Club often gathered for their weekly card games, Sir Alfred put a kettle of water on the mini-stove and motioned for Julian to have a seat at the card table. The flames began to lick at the blackened bottom of the kettle.

As Sir Alfred pulled up a folding chair and loosened his collar, Julian couldn't help but stare up at the ceiling tiles. They were directly under his bedroom, which made Julian wonder just how many secret talks the Elders had had at this very same table. And now, he was taking part in their conversation. Things were just too weird.

The teakettle began to simmer. Sir Alfred wiped his brow tiredly and then locked eyes with Julian. "Years ago, there was a junior member among our ranks named Gabriel," he began.

Julian felt a shiver in his spine at the mention of that name. He wasn't sure why. It didn't make sense. He had never heard it before. But there was something ugly about the way it sounded. The way it made him feel.

Sir Alfred continued, "He was unlike any other Keeper we had ever had. Magnetic, charismatic, promising. So much potential. He not only got noticed by the other juniors, but many of our seniors and even Elders found themselves *entranced* by him."

The water in the kettle began to bubble; making a plop-plopping sound that distracted Julian.

"Of course, not all of us were so entranced."

"Why?" Julian found himself more interested than he expected.

Sir Alfred answered, "He was full of himself. He felt that he could do no wrong. And he was as stubborn as the day is long."

Julian looked away, realizing that he also had been quite stubborn lately.

"At first, I admired Gabriel's conviction. But then, I began to see how he ignored the opinions of others, dismissed the suggestions of the Elders and saw himself as superior. Worse, he openly challenged our authority; even likened himself to the Father."

The water in the kettle bubbled over and the whistle began to shriek. Sir Alfred scooted back his chair and stood to attend to it.

"The Father?" Julian asked,

Sir Alfred took the kettle off the flame. The shrieking whistle stopped abruptly and quiet was restored to the small room. "The originator of time, Julian."

Julian snorted, "You can't be serious? You don't actually mean...Father Time?"

Sir Alfred poured a cup of steaming hot water into two blue cracked mugs, one for himself and one for Julian. "To us, he is just the Father. We leave all other interpretations to storybook writers and civilians."

"Father TIME?" Julian stared at Sir Alfred in disbelief. Now things were getting downright preposterous.

Sir Alfred dropped a teabag into each cup and brought them to the table. "Gabriel was so certain that it was his destiny to lead us all into the future. He told others that one day he would hold ultimate power; that he would essentially replace the Father. He even went as far as to promise everlasting security. After all, he argued, who would dare challenge the Society with him in control of time?

"It was an absurd notion. Even the Father himself refrained from ever using complete power because He understood the importance of leaving mankind to its own free will." Sir Alfred pursed his lips and blew on his tea, patiently waiting for it to cool.

"We all must follow our own path, Julian. The Father knew this. He wanted this. But still, we tolerated the ramblings of this...Gabriel. He was, after all, an asset to the Society. Learned. Inventive. Brave. And his enthusiasm was infectious."

BANG!

Julian jumped. The loud noise was followed by a muffled curse from Bishop downstairs.

WHUMP!

Something had been kicked across the cellar floor. *It better not be one of my inventions*, thought Julian.

Sir Alfred proceeded. "But in order to let him rise in power, we Elders had to be sure of his character. Your granddad secretly tested Gabriel. Many times. And every time, he failed."

Another bang from below. And another curse from Bishop. Had Sir Alfred not heard the ruckus in the cellar?

"Some did not want to accept this truth - that evil was in his blood," Sir Alfred went on, "Sometimes people are born the way they are, Julian. And nothing can be done to change it."

Julian took a sip of tea and burned his lip.

"What happened next was inevitable. Gabriel and his flock of followers waged a war that came to be known as our Second Great Battle. It lasted three moons. Many lives were lost on both sides, and blood spilled from Spain to Egypt and back."

Sir Alfred set down his cup and took Julian's hand in his own.

"But it ended *here*, Julian. *Right here.* In the exact coordinates of that rift in your cellar."

Julian felt frozen, unable to move. What was Sir Alfred saying? It wasn't possible!

"Your granddad must have built that clock around the rift to conceal it, and then this shop above to safeguard its secret from ever being revealed. Freemont knew that sometimes keeping people in the dark was the only way to keep them safe."

For Julian that was a wickedly ironic marriage of thoughts - darkness and safety.

Bishop came thumping up the cellar stairs, his angry mumbles growing louder. "Not good."

Sir Alfred glanced at Bishop, a slightly panicked look passing over his eyes. Sir Alfred locked eyes again with Julian. "Now it seems that Gabriel has devised a way to travel from the dimension of his exile...back home to this one."

Julian whispered to himself, "The Black Taxi."

Suddenly he was filled with dread as the image of the charging taxi flashed again in his mind. How it had stalked him like a bull, dirty steam puffing from its grill. He imagined it blasting through the wall of the Chronus Family Cleaners, catching poor Linus by surprise.

"This isn't just about revenge for being exiled, Julian," Sir Alfred explained. "It is Gabriel's unwavering lust for the Father's supreme power. That's why he's taken your granddad, because he knows Freemont is the only one standing between him and the Sacred Object."

Julian could feel his hands trembling. He hid them under the table. A million thoughts raced through his mind. *Dear God. If that rift is real, then the Society must also be real. And that madman, Gabriel, too. Granddad really is in danger!*

Julian jumped to his feet, knocking over his teacup and spilling hot tea all over him. He barely felt the pain. All he could think about was Granddad. "We must get help. We have to call someone!" Julian dug into the front pocket of his short pants and produced Detective Riley's business card.

Bishop watched him, unimpressed.

Julian rushed to the wall phone, lifted the receiver and began punching away at the numbers.

Suddenly, a stubby index finger depressed the phone cradle button. The line went dead. "When are you going to stop running to everyone else for help, boy?" Bishop asked quietly.

Julian was speechless. He shrugged his shoulders limply and sat back down.

"Now, Bishop—" Sir Alfred had become fond of the stubborn boy, much to his surprise.

"The answers you seek are right here," Bishop continued sternly. "Beginning with that rift you so cleverly discovered downstairs. *That's* the key to saving your granddad, and the only way to stop Gabriel from forcing your grandfather to reveal the location of the Sacred Object."

"How do you possibly know that?" Julian couldn't believe he was actually asking this question. "How do you know what's on the other side of that rift? There could be green space aliens in there for all you know." Julian looked at both men, waiting for some answer that made sense of it all.

Sir Alfred smiled warmly. "We know that rift will lead to Gabriel's dimension because it was that very rift that took him from ours." Sir

Alfred stood up and adjusted his tweed blazer with purpose. “We must go. We must save your granddad before Gabriel gets the information from him. Trust me, Julian. We can’t let that happen.” Sir Alfred nodded for Bishop to open the cellar door.

“I think the *we* part is where things get a bit sticky,” Bishop warned over his shoulder.

Julian frowned. He didn’t like the sound of that. “How do you mean?”

“The rift,” Bishop shot back, “It’s getting smaller.”

“It’s – shrinking?” Julian sat up in alarm.

“Like a cut on the skin of this dimension, the rift is slowly healing itself,” Bishop said.

Julian laughed nervously. “Turns out that time *does* heal all wounds, huh?”

Neither of the two old men so much as cracked a smile.

Bishop knelt down near Julian, uncomfortably close to the boy. “As a result of that contraction,” Bishop explained carefully, “The rift is simply too small for either me or Sir Alfred to pass through safely. It must be you who goes to the other dimension, Julian.”

Julian lost his balance on the chair, flying backward and falling to the tile floor with a crash. He looked up, “What? Me? No, thank you!”

Sir Alfred approached. “It’s all right, Bishop. I will go alone. I shall just have to take the risk.”

“Then you will die,” replied Bishop plainly. “It is a simple matter of physics. Your demise is almost certain. The manner of your demise is the only variable. You might be atomically stretched like spaghetti as you travel the wormhole, or you might simply implode once you get to the point where the pressure is too great, or any number of other gruesome outcomes may occur. But either way, it will not help you save Freemont – or protect the Sacred Object, as we have sworn to do with our lives.”

Sir Alfred dropped his eyes and nodded reluctantly.

Bishop helped Julian up from the floor. “It must be you, Julian. You are the only one. Take Freemont’s cane with you and use it as your guide. Trust in it as he has done for so many years.”

Julian dusted himself off. “I’m sorry but I am not going anywhere. You are the ‘Keeper of Time’, not me. I’m just a kid. I can’t even keep my room clean.” He approached Sir Alfred and lowered his voice. “You said I had the information inside me to save Granddad. And I’ve given you that, have I not?”

Sir Alfred nodded. "You have, Julian. But I also said that you had much more inside to give and that you must believe it to be so."

Julian walked over to the raised staircase that exposed the cellar and locked it back down in place. "I'm sorry. Truly, I am. But I'm not the man for the job."

NINE

A Tear in Time

Julian fell on his bed yet again. This time, there was no need to force his eyes shut. This time, the weight of the world pulled them down like window shades blocking out the harsh view of reality.

It was only moments before Julian fell fast asleep and into a dream. Not the horrible dream he had suffered through so many other nights, of a world dipped in black and a torch about to lose its flame. No, this was a wonderful dream, the best Julian had ever had.

It was a beautiful autumn day. A light breeze tickled the sunflowers in front of Westminster Academy for Young Men.

It was his first day at the new school and Julian was being dropped off at the main entrance, but he did not sit on the cold seat of a school bus as he had the four years prior at Westminster Under School. No, this time, he was seated in the back seat of the family car, with his mother and father. Even in his dream, Julian could feel his heart tighten with familiar pain and longing. They were a happy family enjoying a happy day.

The car stopped and Julian hopped out. He smiled a confident and cheery smile back at his loving parents.

The beautiful dream continued. A crowd of students gathered before Julian, greeting him with smiles and looks of admiration then parted before him like the Red Sea. Julian felt like the superhero he had promised Lily he would someday be.

And there she was, Lily. Holding the school door for him, her almond eyes lit up. Julian did not question why Lily would be at an Academy for Young Men. He didn't question any of it because it all felt right.

As Julian stepped into the school, he turned for one last look back at his parents. They waved slowly with tears in their eyes before the car faded in the distance. Lily turned and said to Julian in a honey-coated voice, "I was wrong about you, Julian."

She continued to say his name. Louder. Then louder. "Julian. JULIAN!"

Julian woke to blinding morning light pouring through his window. He rubbed his eyes in an effort to acclimate. And the voice still called.

"Julian!"

He stepped over to the window, propped it open and looked down on the cobblestone road to find Lily and Martin staring back in the fresh clothes of a new day.

"You still owe us that drink, Rigby," Lily cracked.

Martin smiled, "And I.O.U. one punch."

Julian rubbed his eyes again, still foggy from his long overdue sleep. "What are you two doing here?"

"What do you mean?" asked Lily, as if insulted by the question. "We are your friends, stupid. We wanted to know what happened to you. We heard you were arrested!"

Julian was stunned. Now he was awake. *Did she just say friends?*

He hadn't had anyone call him that since kindergarten, and even then it was only because his classmate couldn't remember names and called everyone in the class 'friend'.

But here they were. Standing below his bedroom window at the crack of dawn on a summer's day when they could have been anywhere they wanted. That was about the best thing he had seen in a while. For the first time in a long time, Julian smiled without forcing it.

Suddenly, the loud cooing of a familiar white dove hiding in a nearby tree rudely interrupted Julian's moment.

"Shoo, you pesky bird!" he growled.

"Hey!" scolded Lily.

"What? It's a nuisance."

"No, Julian. It's a Mourning Dove. That cooing is said to be their mourning of a lost partner. So have a heart."

Julian rolled his eyes, and then looked at Martin. "Did you really come all this way to make sure I'm okay?"

"I think your arrest boosted your street cred so much that I just may have to think twice about messing with you." Martin smiled.

Julian smiled back down at his new friends and offered his own gift in return. "You guys want to see something?"

It wasn't long before the three of them were carefully tiptoeing past a snoring Bishop and Sir Alfred, who lay sloppily on makeshift beds in the clock shop. Martin looked at the men oddly, but Lily ignored them.

"Isn't it dangerous to let homeless people sleep in your store, Julian?" Martin wondered aloud.

"Shhhh." Julian pushed all of his weight on the bottom step of the stairs, causing it to once again pop open and reveal the secret staircase hidden beneath. He led the others quietly down into the cellar.

Moments later, Lily and Martin were staring at the blue glowing rift, speechless. It had gotten smaller since he had seen it last, Julian realized. A good bit smaller.

Martin turned to his new friend slowly. "So if this rift is the way into the dimension to find your granddad, then what would be the way back?"

Julian thought about that. He assumed it worked both ways, but if that were true, then why hadn't Gabriel arrived in the clock shop cellar? Then it struck him…"The Black Taxi!"

Lily's eyes lit up fascinated. "You mean that strange-looking machine we saw from the bridge?"

"It is how Gabriel returned to our dimension."

The rift's energy floated before them like a magical little solar system of stars and planets orbiting with their own strange logic.

Martin breathed deeply and nodded toward Julian. "I'm in."

Julian laughed, "You're in? For what?"

"For the challenge of saving your granddad, Jules. It's high time this Winkleman earned his own stripes. Besides, this job can't be done without me. You said it yourself that the Black Taxi left no tire tracks at the cleaner's, and that you never saw wheels touch the ground when it nearly struck you."

Julian responded, "So?"

"So...it's likely that it's a *flying* machine, and who else among us comes from a family of aviators?"

Julian waved off the effort. "No, no, no. We're not going anywhere. I just thought it would be cool to show it to you, that's all."

"That's not true," interjected Lily. "Be honest with yourself. Somewhere inside you, you knew that if you showed it to us, we might help you. You want our help, Julian. You need it. Your granddad needs it. And it sounds like the world needs it."

Julian wasn't sure what to think. *Maybe Lily was right.*

"I'm in, too," Lily declared. "Imagine it, Julian. Another dimension in time. The possibilities are endless. There could be unicorns and elves and...such grand adventures! Besides, you said it yourself, Julian. You said that you have a great sense of adventure."

"I was speaking metaphorically. Or sarcastically or...something," Julian stammered.

She pulled at his shirtsleeve. "Think about it. No parents to tell us what we can and cannot do."

Lily caught herself in horror, realizing the insensitivity of her words. "I'm sorry. I'm so sorry. I didn't mean..."

Julian took a moment, then dug into his pocket and pulled out a yellow piece of paper. He unfolded it carefully. Lily and Martin watched him curiously.

The paper was scribbled with a title, 'Things to Avoid Avoiding'.

There was a long list of words such as 'girls', 'spiders', 'darkness', and more. But at the end was a phrase he had added just a day earlier, while sitting alone on the bridge, waiting for them.

It read, 'Being a tourist.'

Lily and Martin waited for a response.

Julian stared back at their faces and realized that they really were his friends now. Only true friends would ever dare put their lives in danger to help you. How lucky he was to have them, he thought.

They stared patiently, waiting for a signal from him until finally..."Super. Looking forward to it."

They lit up with smiles and laughter.

"Shh!" Julian remembered. "You're going to wake up Sir Alfred and Bishop."

Martin laughed, "You mean those two old geezers upstairs?"

Julian couldn't resist laughing along with them.

"When this is all over, we'll be famous." Martin added.

Julian lifted granddad's antique cane. "Look, this is just an in-and-out mission, okay? Bishop told me to use this cane as our guide. It must be some sort of all-purpose tool because it unlocked the family heirloom, too. I'm sure once we get it into Granddad's hands, he'll be able to use it like a compass or something and get us back home before anyone even realizes we were gone."

Lily nodded and Julian moved toward the rift.

"Wait, what about all these gadgets of yours?" Martin asked. "Shouldn't we be prepared?"

Julian looked around the cellar. A smile grew across his funny face. His inventions. Yes. While Lily and Martin nodded encouragement, Julian suited up like Batman. First, the Rigby Knuckle. Then, the Jack-in-the-Watch. And even a few works-in-progress.

Finally, Julian was prepared. "You guys ready?"

"Wait – let me go first," Martin said. "I'll make sure it's safe." Before the other two could even respond, Martin had stepped one leg into the energy field. It glowed bright blue. "Whoa," Martin said, looking back at his friends. "It feels weird. I wonder—"

Suddenly, Martin was completely sucked away into the rift, without another sound.

Lily and Julian stared after their friend, astonished. *And*, Julian thought, *had the rift gotten bigger just then? Like a python that had swallowed a meal?*

"You sure about this?" Julian looked at Lily nervously, but she was already halfway immersed in the rift.

With an eager wave, she beckoned him. "Hurry, Julian! We don't have much...time! Time! Time!" Lily's voice echoed as she disappeared into the whirling vortex.

The rift seemed to expand once again and its glow became brighter. It was like an insatiable beast, feeding on the energy of Martin and Lily.

Julian shook with fear as he tentatively inched his way closer to the glowing mini-universe. *No going back now*, he thought. Clutching Granddad's cane tightly, Julian dipped a toe into the rift as if he were checking the temperature of the water in a pool before deciding to take the plunge.

But no sooner did just the tip of Julian's shoe cross the threshold of the rift, when...

FLOOP!

The scrawny schoolboy was sucked in like plankton into the mouth of a blue whale. Julian's entry however, did not go as quietly or smoothly as that of his friends.

Quite the contrary. When Julian disappeared into the rift, the entire clock shop and apartment above it were shaken with a sonic boom and filled with a blinding light that exploded and collapsed back into itself like a quasar.

Upstairs, Sir Alfred was startled out of his sleep and, in fact, right out of his makeshift bed. He hit the floor with a *whump* and stared at Bishop helplessly. Without words, both men leapt to the doorway and ran downstairs as fast as their spindly old legs could take them.

In only moments, but what seemed an eternity later, the two Keepers stood in the cellar wordlessly, as a pulsing blue glow illuminated them both.

The rift throbbed repeatedly. "He's done the right thing," Bishop nodded.

Sir Alfred answered, "Yes. But have we?"

TEN

Wilfred

Somewhere, in the darkness of a strange world very far away, where the terrain steamed and glowed with unearthly blue-gray hues, Gabriel nudged Freemont forward as they walked along a rocky trail on a treacherous mountain's edge.

His wrists bound behind his back by Gabriel's bullwhip, the old man stumbled. What he wouldn't do for his cane right now.

Moments later, they arrived at the large wooden doors of what looked like an ancient grinding mill. Covered with cobwebs and moss, it leaned crookedly to one side.

"You know that I was unjustly banished, Freemont. It is I who am the victim here." Gabriel spoke cavalierly, as if he were offering an old friend a cup of tea.

Freemont couldn't help but snort at such an absurd notion. "Says the captor to his hostage," growled Freemont.

Gabriel went on. "I was forced into this position. Robbed of my true destiny, and now I am left with no other choice but to fight to claim what is rightfully mine."

With a creak of the heavy wooden doors, the two entered the mill. Freemont now saw why the structure was so crooked – the entire foundation was cracked. He knew, immediately, how it had happened.

Freemont's eyes traced the crack in the dusty concrete slab from his feet all the way to the other side. "You put yourself here, Gabriel. For once in your life, just accept responsibility for your actions."

Gabriel pulled up a rickety metal chair and forced Freemont to have a seat. "Look at us. Can we agree on nothing?" He smiled coyly.

Freemont scanned the open space around him. He saw what appeared to be a workshop. There were metals of all sizes, shapes and colors. Some looked very much like those that constituted the body of the Black Taxi that had brought them to this dimension.

"Let us agree on this, then," Gabriel said. "You tasted victory years ago; now it's my turn."

Freemont clenched his jaw and waited for Gabriel to continue.

"And my victory shall be glorious. I will rise, like a phoenix from the ashes, to rule not only your realm, but also an infinite many more. I will have complete control over time and space.

I will rewrite history. My ascent will be known as the reincarnation of...the Father."

Freemont could not believe what he was hearing. "You – you are mad!"

"Madness, genius...what's the difference, really?"

Freemont looked around with panic, hoping to find some sort of way out of this mess.

It did not go unnoticed. "Please, Monty. Don't insult me by trying to escape. There's nowhere to go. The entire island is under my control, and surrounded by waterfalls that spill into, well, nowhere. A great abyss. Quite strange, really. So let's just agree that Plan A isn't worth the effort, shall we?"

"And what of your flying craft you've just crashed in the hills?" Freemont asked.

Gabriel chuckled, "Come, come, old chap. We both know you haven't the skills to fix my machine. It's not some simple clock that you can just fiddle back together. You never had my gift for such inventions."

"There are many qualities we do not share, Gabriel," responded Freemont, "And that sits quite well with me."

Gabriel smiled from ear to ear, his grimy teeth proudly revealed. He found their exchange most entertaining. "You know, there was a time when you respected my hubris. I dare say some of your people even encouraged it."

Suddenly, something dawned on Freemont. He smiled at his captor, a sight that made Gabriel's eyes narrow in suspicion.

"What's so funny?"

"That Black Taxi of yours. You were forced to build it, weren't you? Because you couldn't find your way back through the rift. How many years did you search this dimension for the portal? I see now why you've gone even madder than before, boy."

Gabriel's nostrils flared and his white eyes narrowed dangerously once more. "Careful who you call boy, geezer." Gabriel's jaw clenched but it did nothing to scare Freemont.

"That's the downside to being so intelligent, isn't it Gabriel? It frustrates you to no end when you can't solve a problem." Freemont was under Gabriel's skin now, dancing on a delicate nerve. "You pondered it, searched for it, toiled over it. But where did it get you? Failure. An all-too-familiar companion of yours."

Gabriel's smiled dropped and his face turned hard. Freemont persisted, "And you fancy yourself the reincarnation of the Father? You're not fit to wash his robe, child."

Gabriel reached out his leather-gloved hand and grabbed Freemont by his wrinkly face, squeezing, and spoke softly into the old man's ear. "If you think you or anyone else in the Society could have done better here, you're greatly mistaken. I searched this sky for eons. That portal is gone."

Gabriel let go of Freemont's face and smoothed out his flight suit with satisfaction. He continued proudly, "And who cares, anyway? I built a machine that can take me back not only to your dimension but also to any other I desire. So keep your rift, your rules, your Keepers' Bible and vows. They're of no use to me."

Gabriel looked at the large crack in the floor pointedly. "I think it's time we get on with what we're here for. Wilfred!" Gabriel called into the crack. "Wilfred, my friend. I have a job for you."

He turned back to Freemont. "You will enjoy Wilfred. Like you ridiculous Keepers, he also has a hopeless appreciation for the rhyme." Suddenly, from the darkness of the crack came an echo of a delightful, little voice.

"Who does call me on this day?
Is it my sire, come my way?
I am humbled, I must say.
And do so hope you enjoy your stay."

From out of the crack, a small, green, fuzzy creature wriggled. As it came closer, clearing a path through the dust on the floor, Freemont realized quickly it was a caterpillar, and an interesting one at that.

Wilfred wore thick glasses and a harness strapped to his long, wiggly body that supported tiny paper-thin wooden wings.

"What have you been up to now, little Wilfred?" asked Gabriel, amused by his hopeless harness and wings.

Wilfred peered up through his goggles with magnified eyes.

"What you see is my latest work.
A caterpillar with an *extra* perk.
These wings will wing me into flight.
Just one more test to make them right."

"Oh, Wilfred. When will you stop with your gimmicks and gadgets? Take it from me, they will only disappoint you in the end."

Wilfred forced an embarrassed smile. Gabriel couldn't help but laugh at him. "So pitiful, but I adore you," Gabriel condescended.

Wilfred bowed his head respectfully.

"Your majesty, what may I do?
I exist to serve only you."

Gabriel turned to Freemont with a smile on his face. “See that? That’s called respect, Monty. Wilfred, my most loyal subject, I have for you a great opportunity to serve both your king and your kingdom.”

Wilfred glanced over at Freemont, now bound in his chair by the bullwhip.

Freemont felt a kindred spirit in the little caterpillar’s magnified eyes. After all, they both were prisoners here.

Wilfred turned reluctantly back to his master.

“Ask it of me now, my Lord.
And I shall act to your accord.”

Wilfred bowed low, and then pushed himself back up again with effort.

Freemont watched the little one curiously. He wasn’t sure what Gabriel was about to ask of the creature, but he knew it wasn’t going to be good for either of them.

Gabriel crouched down closer to Wilfred. “It is an exciting day for us both, little caterpillar,” he began. “I have discovered a way to restore Delphisola back to its former glory.”

Wilfred's little eyes flickered with hope. He stiffened up for a tick then promptly wiggled out of his hopeless contraption of wings.

"Is it true, m'lord?
Restart anew, m'lord?"

Gabriel stretched out an open palm and laid it down next to Wilfred to climb aboard. "It is true."

Wilfred stepped onto Gabriel's grimy glove with glee. He sang joyously, while Gabriel smiled and hummed along.

"Rejoice. Rejoice, Delphisolans.
For time will soon resume again.
The flowers will bloom. The suns will rise."

Gabriel playfully finished his little tune...

"And caterpillars will meta-morph-o-size."

Wilfred delightedly gasped at the thought of it. To finally make the change. His change. Wilfred was giddy with excitement.

"Your time to mature has come, little one. Time at last to fly," Gabriel promised.

A tiny tear trickled down Wilfred's fuzzy little face and fell into the blackness of the crack in the floor.

"But in order to do this," Gabriel said. "I will need your help."

"Anything, your majesty," Wilfred answered in his tiny voice.

Gabriel's face turned sour as he glared at Freemont. "This man hides the information we need to make our dreams come true."

Freemont shook his head. He knew it was all lies and couldn't sit still for it. He looked solemnly down at Wilfred and spoke calmly to the little one. "He came to your island and things changed."

Wilfred did not answer Freemont. He was afraid to. Freemont continued. "The land cracked and time stopped. Is that it?"

Wilfred stared at Freemont oddly. How could this man know that—

RRIIIIP!

Gabriel tore a rag in half and glowered at Freemont, who went on.

"Then he subjugated all this world's inhabitants and now rules as your dark master. Think about that, little friend. Why would he want to change that?"

"Enough, liar!" Gabriel stuffed the rag into Freemont's mouth, silencing the old man.

"Wilfred, he is the one who caused the disturbance in this realm that cracked the island and stopped time. And he has the information to reverse it. You must believe me."

Wilfred nodded, growing a bit skeptical.

"Go, Wilfred. Go into his ear and travel his mind. Find and extract the secret of the Sacred Object. It will be hidden in the deepest recesses. That is the assignment your king gives you. Will you accept? Will you save Delphisola?"

Swallowing a nervous lump, Wilfred nodded back in agreement.

Gabriel patted the caterpillar's little head, inadvertently knocking his glasses sideways. "They will tell tales of you from the Enchanted Forests to the Hills of Gaspar."

Gabriel wrapped an arm around Freemont's head, holding it still, and with his other hand he guided Wilfred up and into Freemont's ear. "Your destiny awaits, Wilfred," he said.

Wilfred shook nervously, but into the dark canal he went, traversing a complicated labyrinth of twists and turns.

Gabriel guided him from outside, "That's it, Wilfred. Do not concern yourself with all that you see in those outer layers. Those are but the unlocked, unprotected memories that swirl around so freely."

And he did see them. Many of them. Floating aimlessly like bubbles.

Wilfred saw Freemont proudly hanging the sign outside the AM/PM Emporium. He saw the Bridge Club sharing a laugh over a card game in the dimly lit back room of the clock shop. And he watched Freemont whistle merrily while tending to each of his clocks in the morning, starting with the large 24-Hour Glass and ending with his delicate, miniature Big Ben.

"Click clock, tickety-tock," the old man sang.

"Venture deep into his mind, little Wilfred," coaxed Gabriel.

Freemont could feel each step of Wilfred's sixteen tiny feet wiggling through his mind. It felt like an itch he could not scratch. He twitched, tried to shake his head wildly.

Inside, Wilfred slid and tumbled but kept on going. He knew that his mission was bigger than his fears.

"Look for the darkest cracks and crevices, Wilfred. The memory we seek will be hidden well," Gabriel guided.

Wilfred's little voice echoed back out from Freemont's ear. "Sire, Sire!...

"I think that I have just now found.
A way around the lights and sound."

Freemont bit down on the cloth stuffed in his mouth. His eyes burned into the white pupils of his foe.

"Enter, Wilfred. Do not fear. Your bravery will save us all," Gabriel encouraged.

Wilfred nudged a piece of the wall in Freemont's mind, revealing a passageway that he slid down, whirling and turning until he landed in a foggy, open space where images, sounds and scenes all scattered like bats from a cave, disturbed by some visitor not meant to be there.

"I see them now. Each memory.
They try to escape the very eyes of me."

Gabriel's dirty grin grew large. Softly, he whispered to Wilfred, "Now, my most loyal subject...tell me what you see."

ELEVEN

A Mind Full of Secrets

Swords clanged, flags waved, smoke swirled, shouts rang out and horse hooves thundered. Everything was happening at once in the midst of a pitched battle deep inside Freemont's memory.

And Wilfred was right in the middle of it.

Freemont's memory slowed, blurred, then stretched its wings and fluttered away. Wilfred watched, amazed.

Faintly, Wilfred heard Gabriel's impatient voice. "Hurry, Wilfred!"

But Wilfred was too bewildered to respond. Besides, he had to find out *where* in Freemont's memory resided the secret that Gabriel said would set Delphisola free. The secret of the Sacred Object.

Wilfred stepped forward slowly and cautiously as winged memories swooped and fluttered all around him. It was as if he were flying through a storm of music and color. Fly. That is what Wilfred yearned to do. But that wasn't going to happen unless he found the memory that Gabriel sought.

Something fluttered close to Wilfred's fuzzy body. He turned only to be immersed again in another vivid memory.

Whoosh!

A rapier seemed to graze Wilfred. It was another battle, this time between only two men.

Freemont, middle-aged, strong and confident, was dressed in chain mail covering a white vestment. "I am hoping not to use this, Gabriel," this younger Freemont shouted.

Gabriel, also with a younger face and the infinity clock insignia on his black leather vest, drew his sword as well. "Funny. I was actually hoping for quite the opposite." Gabriel pointed his sword at a small, wooden rectangular box that lay between the two men. "Unless..."

"Never!" cried Freemont with more volume and passion than Wilfred could register through his fuzzy little ears.

"Give me the box, Freemont. I need the Sacred Object."

The warrior Freemont remained silent and instead pointed his sword at Gabriel, as a final warning to his opponent.

Gabriel lunged, with his sword high in the air, at Freemont, who blocked the blow, deflecting a double-edged blade that missed him and instead struck the precious, rectangular wooden box.

Wilfred cowered at the memory before him, which suddenly turned into a blindingly bright supernatural explosion!

"Wilfred, what's happening?" Gabriel's voice drifted in once more from the outside. Gabriel stared at the twitching and itching Freemont still bound to the chair by his bullwhip, his eyes as hard as stones. "Any minute now, Monty," Gabriel grinned, menacingly. "I'll discover your secrets."

Dejected, Freemont sadly closed his eyes and he unwillingly shared the next memory with Wilfred.

The blinding explosion was recurring. Only this time, Wilfred watched in terror as it sent a ripple of pure, electric energy across the landscape. It headed toward the figures of a man and a woman, huddled in fear.

In another flash, the couple vaporized completely.

A tear ran down Freemont's cheek as he was forced to reflect upon the painful memory again, along with Wilfred.

Gabriel shouted, "What is it, Wilfred? What did you see?"

Wilfred gulped.

“A pain so deep – I have not seen
As with *this* man, within this scene
A spirit crushed to no end
A broken heart that may never mend.”

“Yes, but what do you SEE, you stupid insect!” Gabriel was almost jumping out of his skin with impatience.

Wilfred peered into the quickly disappearing memory but it seemed to be over. Except—

“I see a mark in the air. It’s throbbing. It’s...” Wilfred was staring at something very odd indeed. “—A humming, pink, blue ball of energy of some kind. Like a miniature universe. Like—”

“Yes, caterpillar. It is the rift caused by the explosion when I struck the box. I am quite familiar with it, thank you. But what of the wooden box? Tell me what is inside that box!”

Wilfred searched the blurry memory for the box. It was in the arms of the younger Freemont, who stood still as a stone as he stared at the place where the young couple had dematerialized into nothingness.

Wilfred wept. He had never felt such raw emotion.

The young warrior Freemont turned toward the young Gabriel filled with the rage of a thousand men. He gripped the handle of his

Keeper's sword and raised it high, ready to charge. But he didn't have to.

The force of Freemont's wrath itself created another energy ripple, this one so powerful that it struck Gabriel like a tidal wave of air sending him stumbling backwards – and *into* the mysterious rift.

With a sucking, whistling noise, Gabriel disappeared, first one arm, then another, then a leg that twisted upon entry, and worst of all, leaving a horrid scream that echoed long after he was gone.

"THE BOX, WILFRED!" Gabriel shouted from outside the swirling memory chamber of Freemont's head.

But the memory was over. It fluttered away like a moth toward some brighter light. Wilfred found himself smiling, just slightly, at the justice earned by Gabriel. And it explained much to the little creature, how the Dark One had been banished from his own world and into this one.

"I know not much, of your kind,"

Wilfred said, as he clambered back out of Freemont's ear and into Gabriel's dirt-encrusted hands.

Gabriel nodded, seemingly annoyed by this game.

“But this one here, you must unbind.
For he is good. His honor true.
Wronged through time by the likes of you.”

“Careful, bug. Let’s focus on what was in that wooden box, lest we find ourselves saying things we might regret,” Gabriel warned.

But for the first time ever, Wilfred found in himself the courage to stand up to the Dark One. “Very well,” he answered.

“There was a ripple, in your land.
Two were killed. Two left to stand.
Upon that sacred box you struck,
The blame for death is yours, not luck.”

SMASH!

Gabriel’s fist slammed down atop the little caterpillar without warning. When he lifted his leathery glove, all that was left were the shattered lenses from Wilfred’s tiny glasses. “Eternal darkness it shall be, my little wingless friend,” Gabriel sneered.

Freemont bowed his head. He could not have been any more ashamed of what Gabriel had become. "Believe me, Gabriel, when I tell you that no man has been made to suffer the realities of this truth more than I, no man more tested to obey it. Yet still, its truth remains...time is not for man to control, it is merely for us to protect."

"Blah, blah, blah," mocked Gabriel.

Freemont continued, "Let me put it another way. There will be no victory of any kind in your endeavors to learn of the Sacred Object – not today, not tomorrow, or any infinite days thereafter. I will never allow you to discover it."

"Oh, don't be so sure about that," replied Gabriel as he lifted Freemont from the chair and nudged the old man back out of the mill and onto the mossy path. "After all, you always said I had a knack for surprises... Father."

TWELVE

Journey to the Other Side

Julian's mind was racing. So was his body. Eyes open wide in a mixture of panic and awe; Julian was streaking like a bullet down a blindingly bright tube. His whole body jerked to the right as the tunnel took a smeared, cobalt blue left turn at full throttle.

Julian noticed that he wasn't breathing. It was as if he were in a tunnel through the stars, which had no atmosphere. Even though he seemed to be moving faster than he thought possible, not a hair was out of place. Julian was perfectly still, and yet streaking through a kaleidoscope of colors, sensations and images. Numbers and figures melted and warped like those on Headmaster Benson's infinity clock.

As he whirled along, Julian began to feel a pulling sensation at his feet and head. *It must be the spaghettification process Bishop spoke of*, he thought. It was only mildly painful, but enough to remind him to tuck in as tightly as he could, making himself as small as possible.

Julian held onto Granddad's cane, resisting a pulling force that seemed to grasp at it. He crossed his hands and legs over the cane protectively. He would sooner lose a limb than the very thing Granddad needed to save them all.

Suddenly, everything stopped – *POW!* Julian felt as if he had been hurled out of a brightly lit canon at high velocity into darkness, and silence.

Like a newborn sucking in its first breath, Julian's lungs filled with a foreign, stale air and his limbs flailed as he fell.

And fell. And fell.

Why haven't I landed yet? He panicked. *How long could this fall last? And where in Heaven's name will I land?*

His free fall, narrated by the sounds of his own screams, was interrupted by an even louder shout from below. "Julian!" screamed two voices.

"Martin? Lily?" he shouted back. "How long have you been falling?" Julian hollered down.

"Too long!" answered Martin.

Julian's eyes finally began to adjust to his whereabouts, but his new surroundings offered little information other than a slight purple glow from above. "What should we do?" he called back down.

"Curl in a ball and hope for the best," answered Lily.

Suddenly, there were two loud splashes below.

"Guys?" he cried out.

Then, Julian was smacked by a wall of tepid, soupy water that assaulted every part of his body. The impact knocked Granddad's cane free from his grip. "No!" he shouted, as he frantically tried to swim after it.

"Help, I can't swim!" screamed Lily from nearby.

Julian turned away from the cane to find Lily already being rescued by Martin who expertly held her with one arm and paddled with the other.

"Have you got her?" Julian asked.

"I'm a Winkleman. We're born Olympians. Now go get that cane."

Julian turned back to find Granddad's cane drifting away in the soupy water dappled with a golden glow. Could it be...moonlight?

Julian didn't have time to find out. The cane was drifting farther and farther out of reach.

As Martin brought Lily safely to the nearest bit of land, Julian swam through the water toward the cane, trying not to panic, but it wasn't easy.

Lily and Martin ran alongside him on a rocky ridge.

"You're going too fast, Julian!" called Lily.

"It's not me," he shouted back, "It's the current!" Then something horribly slimy brushed against his leg. Julian screamed, "What the heck was that?"

It happened again, brushing his other side. It felt like a slimy eel or stingray. He shuddered at the thought of either one.

Each time it brushed him, Julian became more distracted from retrieving the cane. But he had to reach it quickly – the current was carrying it away faster than he could swim!

Under the rushing purple water, a larger slimy thing twined around his chest and grasped him firmly.

Julian slowed down to almost a standstill, despite the swift current. *What's got hold of me?* He began to panic.

In a desperate attempt to recover himself, Julian splashed wildly. His right arm flailed madly into broad, slippery underwater leaves. *Some kind of seaweed,* he thought, beginning to take hold of the situation.

A vine wrapped itself around his right leg. Then another around his left. Only Julian's right arm was still free. The water rose to his chin and inched higher. Soon he wouldn't be able to breathe!

Lily spotted him from the ridge, "Julian, are you okay?"

"Do I look okay?" he yelled back, completely tangled and beginning to gulp the salty, tepid water that tasted like something that should come from science class.

"Use the Rigby Knuckle!" Martin added.

That's right! Julian thought. He dug down into the water with his free hand and twisted the belt buckle clockwise, unlatching the four-piece survival knife shaped like a Chinese star. He pulled it above the water, chose the serrated 'Buck Knife' option, and then started sawing away at the seaweed.

Suddenly, bubbles began surfacing from the water all around Julian, releasing a high-pitched shrieking sound as they popped. Like a thousand lobsters boiling in a pot, it was a horrible noise. If Julian had had two free hands, he would have covered both ears just to shut out the sound.

Then, as if panicking, the leafy vines slithered around his slim body like ten pythons tightening their grip.

Julian's eyes and mouth were agape in horror. "It's alive!" he screamed, "The seaweed is alive!"

Up on the ridge, Martin could not believe what he had heard. "What does he mean, alive?"

Julian, now completely bound by the seaweed, was no longer moving with the current. The warm purple water slammed against his skinny frame as if he were the pole of a dock during a storm. Small whirlpools formed around his body, held firmly by the seaweed. *Don't panic,* Julian thought. *Just don't panic.* But the more he tried to cut himself free, the more Julian heard those awful bubbly screams, and the tighter the vines gripped him.

Lily watched as the golden glint of moonlight on the handle of Granddad's cane guided her eye along its path, and what she saw then filled her heart with dread. "Stop cutting! Tell him to stop cutting!" she shouted at Martin.

"But he'll be strangled!" panicked Martin.

"Just do it!"

Martin did as he was told, cupping his hands and calling down to Julian. "Let it tangle you, Jules!" he screamed.

Julian stopped just long enough to see what Lily had seen...a roaring waterfall just a few feet away. A faint lilac mist rose up from the churning water and Julian could hear it thundering louder and louder.

He thought to himself, *This is it. This is going to be the end.*

The seaweed seized this opportunity to wrap its last vine around his free hand, taking total control of the boy. The seaweed began to pull and tug on Julian forcefully.

"Ow! Help!" he screamed into the inky violet nothingness that seemed to envelop him like fog. Was he underwater?

"Julian! You're almost there!" Martin's voice rang out.

Suddenly, Julian felt mossy mud beneath him. He had been carried to shore. The seaweed had saved him. Like the powerful tentacles of a great octopus, it had carried Julian all the way back against the raucous current to the ridge of land where his friends waited for him.

"Julian! Here!" Martin reached out his hand and pulled his friend to shore.

Lily looked down at Julian and smiled. "You're okay," she sighed with relief.

"No I'm not." On his back, an utterly bereft Julian added forlornly. "I lost the cane. Granddad's cane." He stared dejectedly up into the strange sky, examining a large, golden full moon orbited by three purple crescent moons, and a black crow that circled above him. The bird reminded Julian of the white Mourning Dove that had sat cooing on his windowsill back at the apartment. He wanted to shoo this one away, too.

The stars began to blur. A single tear streamed down his cheek. Julian wiped it away angrily.

Suddenly one of the constellations shaped like a butterfly moved – very slowly. Julian's jaw dropped as he watched it gracefully flutter its elegant wings and fly away, across the universe. Julian sat up. "Did you see that?"

The three friends stared up at the strange night sky. The moons took up a great deal of the dark horizon. Beyond them, brilliant constellations glittered.

The friends peered and squinted, trying to make out the shapes. But that was almost impossible. The constellations seemed to pulse and dance elegantly and quietly to a song only they could hear.

"A peacock!" Julian pointed. The constellation's peacock feathers first fanned out, then became a hurricane of glittering dust, and finally drifted away. Then another constellation began to take shape.

"Is that – ?" Martin stuttered.

"Is that your granddad?" Lily whispered in awe.

Julian couldn't believe his eyes. The constellation took the form of Freemont, all right. But something was wrong. The figure stumbled and limped. Granddad was in trouble.

The constellation clouded into stardust and began to take on other forms swiftly: a caterpillar, a butterfly, and a bud blossoming into a flower and dying again, stones skipping over water.

"What the – " Martin was rooted to the spot, his neck craned back.

As one of the three purple crescent moons turned blue, the stars continued their mysterious dance.

"What was that all about?" Lily asked, concerned.

But Julian didn't have time to answer. With a splash, something landed next to him. Granddad's cane! The friends stared back at the violet lake from which it had come. A slithering leafy tentacle disappeared under the water.

Julian picked up the cane and smiled with determination. "We're back in business."

The friends nodded in agreement. Julian looked around to take in their new world. The moons allowed him enough light to see that they were high up on some sort of hill. Beyond the hill, only flat darkness. But – what was that? Another light glinted and glittered like diamonds within the darkness.

"It looks like we're on an island," Martin said, a step ahead of Julian. Indeed, the glints of light were riding the dark, silky waves of a great lake.

Together the friends surveyed the land around them more closely. There were sheer rocky drop-offs in every direction. Some were covered with moss, others with strange pink glittering lichen. To the left, far off in the distance, were orange flecks of what looked to be the embers of many fires.

"What do you suppose those lights are, over there?" Julian asked the others.

"Too far to say," Martin answered.

Lily interrupted, "Look. Down there."

A plume of grey smoke snaked its way up into the air from the base of the hill as if it were an ornate Chinese New Year dragon. Sparks danced within it.

Lily smiled with excitement, pondering the possibilities of their new adventure. "Maybe it's from the chimney of a gentle, little elf's home as he cooks porridge over the fire."

Martin groaned. "Sure. Or it could be the smoke from the nostrils of a fire-breathing dragon napping before its next hunt."

Julian shook off the water from his clothes and hair and sighed at this strange, new world dipped in black. *Ugh, why did we have to arrive at night?* Julian stiffened. "Um, guys?" he started—

The three friends watched fearfully as the smoke cleared, allowing the object below to take an eerily familiar form.

THIRTEEN

The Lady in Red

The friends staggered back a few steps, then looked over the edge again.

"I can't believe it," Lily coughed.

It was the Black Taxi, smoking, sparking and utterly crashed against the edge of a boulder.

"Granddad!" Julian sprinted down the hill, falling, rolling and getting back up again as fast as he could.

The three friends hurried toward the smoking monster at the bottom of the hill.

Along the way, Julian passed increasingly stranger things that, in his rush to the Black Taxi, he did not notice. Things his friends, however, did notice.

Un-bloomed flowers of electric colors imprisoned beneath a layer of frost, despite there not being enough cold to warrant it. An eerie stillness in the air interrupted only by what

Martin would swear was a whisper that followed them in the grass.

Breathless, Julian looked inside the Black Taxi, coughing. "Granddad? You in there?" He peered through every window only to find the vehicle empty. Relieved but confused, he stepped back from the smoke and flames.

"You know what this means, don't you?" asked Martin, encouraged. "It means your granddad and his captor have crashed."

Lily knew where Martin was going with this logic and became excited too. "It means they have to be on foot! Which gives us the chance to track them and catch up before they get to…well, wherever they are going."

Julian nodded. It did make sense. He looked down at his feet, planted on the strange, mossy and gravelly ground. The wind was sucked from his sails with the realization, "Our footsteps don't leave tracks here."

The other two friends looked down. It was true. As soon as they stepped into the soil, it sprung back up as if it had never been trodden.

"I have an idea," blurted Martin.

The Black Taxi's smoke was nearly gone now. Martin reached into the driver's window and pulled the lever for the hood, which popped up accordingly. He lifted the hood higher and propped it open with the rod to get a better look.

What Martin, Lily and Julian saw was an engine unlike any they'd ever seen before. Tubes made from what seemed to be the intestines of an animal, an engine block carved from the heavy bark of a tree, anti-freeze that boiled orange like bubbling lava, a curious bundle of the finest feathers as smooth as silk; white feathers that were laced with a shimmering gold dust.

Lily ran her finger along the edge of the feathers, so fair and delicate. They left the same sparkly residue on her fingertips. "It tingles!" she marveled.

"Hope this wasn't our only ride home," Julian worried.

"Home? And where would that be, darlings?"

The three friends jumped back and whipped their heads around, searching for the source of the mysterious voice. It wasn't a familiar voice that answered. It was an older, female voice, as dainty and practiced as that of a ritzy socialite.

Zzzzzzz

Something like a tiny helicopter buzzed by their three amazed faces.

Zzzzzzz

It was a ruby-red ladybug, and it was eyeballing them from head to toe with long, fluttering eyelashes. She was as proper as a royal wedding.

"Who wants to know?" answered Martin.

"Why, everyone, darling. It isn't every day that visitors arrive on Delphisola. Folks'll surely get to talking," the ladybug fluttered.

"Delphisola? Is that what your world is called?" asked Lily, barely able to contain herself.

"It is hardly mine," the ladybug responded, as she buzzed uncomfortably close to Lily's face.

"Listen, ladybug. We haven't much time..." Julian began.

The ladybug suddenly zzzzzz-ed up to Julian's face, eye-to-eye with the startled boy. "Why do you offend me, creature?" She batted her long eyelashes so close that they tickled his nose.

Julian was perplexed. "Sorry?" He took a step back from the fluttering red insect.

"As you should be," she replied. "Lady Beetle, yes. Lady Bird, yes. Lady in Red, yes. But not...ladybug. Ugh, what a dreadful way to address a lady."

"I meant no offense," Julian tried not to roll his eyes, "...Lady in Red."

The ladybug curtsied regally, mid air. "You are forgiven."

Julian did roll his eyes this time, but only Lily noticed. "How do we find the operator of this craft?" She decided to try to distract both of them.

But the ladybug ignored Lily, fluttering around Julian's wrist. "What is that?" she asked.

"It's a watch," Julian answered.

"That's what I thought." The ladybug giggled, spinning in circles like a plane in an air show. "You will find no use for that here, creature."

"What is that supposed to mean?" Julian asked.

The ladybug fluttered just before his nose, her shiny red body with perfectly round black spots. She smelled faintly of roses and honeysuckle. "It's a little known secret that you can tell how old a Lady Beetle is by counting her spots," she answered.

"Now what are you talking about?" asked Julian, growing impatient with her. He had to find Granddad and Gabriel, and fast.

"Of course, a lady never tells her age," the ladybug went on, unperturbed by Julian's growing irritation, "But I've had the same number of spots for as long as I can recall. I'd be happy to let you count."

"I'm not interested in counting your spots. Or chatting. I'm interested in finding my grandfather."

The ladybug remained quiet for a moment. The only sounds were those of her softly beating wings and, far away, the very dull rush of the waterfalls that ringed this strange island.

Then, after a pause, the ladybug resumed speaking. "Afraid I can't help you there, darling. Except to warn – I mean – *encourage* you to return to your own land, and forget this place. Forever."

"What do you mean?" Lily asked. But the sound of the softly beating wings disappeared, along with its owner.

"What do we do now?" Martin asked.

"I think we should find somewhere to hide for the night," Julian answered. "I don't trust the creatures of this island. In the morning, we can travel much more safely by daylight." Julian spotted a shallow cavern that looked like just as good a place as any to retreat for the night.

Lily and Martin followed doubtfully, but Lily spoke up. "We can't wait until morning, Julian, my parents will have all of London looking for me," she explained.

Martin added, "Plus, we'll lose their trail."

"What trail, Martin? We haven't found any evidence of a trail. We don't even know if we're walking in the right direction."

Martin stopped in his footsteps. "Do I need to remind you what's at stake here, Jules? You said yourself that if we don't get that cane to your granddad before Gabriel learns the location of the Sacred Object, then time - as we know it - will be in jeopardy. In this dimension, in our dimension and in every one between."

"Yes, I understand the gravity of what's at stake. But I'm just saying that it would be more prudent to travel by sunlight since we know nothing of this dimension. That's all."

Martin looked puzzled. "What is it you're afraid of, Julian?" he asked, growing suspicious. "Is it failure? Success? The dark?"

Julian's face turned pale and Martin knew he was on to something.

"You're letting a fear of the dark get between us and saving your granddad?" Martin persisted.

Lily immediately felt like she was right back in London, stuck between the two boys as they bickered back and forth.

Julian walked up to Martin, visibly upset. "Do you want to hear that I'm afraid, Third? Will that make things better for you?" Julian pointed

Granddad's cane at Martin. "Fine, then. I'm afraid of the dark. Are you happy now?"

Julian felt the pressure of his daunting mission crushing him. "Anything else you want me to admit I'm afraid of? Okay, how about live seaweed and talking beetles? They kind of creep me out."

He turned his eyes on Lily, "And you? Anything you want to hear me say? That I'm afraid of being lost here? That I'm afraid of adventure? Of being a tourist in someone else's world?"

He whirled Granddad's cane around himself madly, like the conductor of an orchestra, losing himself in his own tantrum. "What else? Let's see...I'm afraid of falling, drowning, choking, burning. I'm afraid of not fitting in. I'm afraid of fitting in. I'm afraid of dying. Of living. And I'm afraid of my own stupid shadow, which is towering over us right now on that wall." He panted. He had finally tired himself out.

Lily and Martin were speechless. Once again, Martin regretted pushing Julian so far. "I'm sorry, Jules. I didn't mean to—"

"Shh, listen!" interrupted Lily.

A strange noise was approaching. It was like the sound of the wind in the trees, only—

"Are those – voices?" Lily looked toward her friends, worried.

The sound grew closer, and mixed in with it was the sound of whispers.

"They're just echoes," Martin answered.

But Lily wasn't so sure. "No, listen!" Lily insisted. "The echoes…they are different from your words. Different from your voices. They are someone else's conversation."

Julian, Lily and Martin all stood frozen as they strained their ears. Then they heard it again. It wasn't the echo of Julian's rant. It was a voice that slowly grew louder. A voice that was smoky and dark.

It was the most horrible voice they had ever heard.

FOURTEEN

Message in a Bottle

In the cellar of the AM/PM Emporium, Sir Alfred stared deep into the throbbing, pulsing, dazzling center of the rift, which now had grown slightly bigger than before.

"It's gotten bigger. I can almost fit," noted Sir Alfred aloud.

"No, old friend. It's been disturbed by Julian's passing through it. It's unstable and grows irregularly," Bishop corrected. "Julian is on his own. We must now think what we can do, for the cause, over here."

Sir Alfred shook his head and took a seat on an empty milk crate. "All we can do now is wait."

Bishop sighed and set Petey down. "We wait? That's it? But what if he doesn't..."

Sir Alfred turned and gave Bishop a look that stopped him cold.

Some things are better left unsaid, he realized. After all, the bond Sir Alfred had with the boy had grown, and he knew his friend worried for Julian as he might his own grandson. Bishop changed course. "Sir Alfred, let's not be dangerously optimistic. He is just a boy, after all."

Petey started chewing on Sir Alfred's morning slipper like a puppy. Oddly, Sir Alfred didn't mind. He did not shake the fuzzy ferret off the way he normally would have. In fact, he did not respond to the creature at all.

He did, however, become quite annoyed by its owner. Sir Alfred stood to face Bishop directly. "Are you saying that you don't believe in him, Bishop?"

Bishop pulled Petey back, with a piece of Sir Alfred's slipper still in his teeth. "Are you saying that you do?" the scientist replied.

Sir Alfred wanted to answer that question as confidently and quickly as he could, but he forced himself to pause and allow both his heart and his mind to agree on the answer. "I believe – that Julian has the potential to succeed. I just never thought he'd have to do it alone."

Bishop watched Petey sniffing around the powdery dust that had fallen earlier from the family heirloom. Bishop noticed something strange. "I am not so sure that he did, Sir Alfred."

Sir Alfred looked down to where Bishop was gesturing. There, in the dust, were footprints. Several different sets of footprints. Sir Alfred swelled with a mixture of emotions. Though he was pleased to discover Julian had not traveled alone, at the same time he was baffled by the thought of whom on Earth Julian had found to accompany him.

Bishop placed his hand over the sets of footprints to measure their size and held it up for Sir Alfred to understand just how small they were. His normally stiff upper lip cracked a grin, "It looks like our little loner has found himself a few friends."

Sir Alfred wiped his moist brow with the back of his hand. "It should have been us by his side, Bishop."

"And it would have been, if it were at all physically possible." Bishop patted Petey on the head for another job well done and nudged him to scamper back up the stairs, then rose back to his feet, careful not to bump his head on the ceiling beams. "Listen, mate. Even with a company of friends, our little Julian still has an enormous task ahead. We cannot go about just waiting and hoping that he may succeed. There is too much at stake. We must have an insurance policy."

Sir Alfred looked longingly back at the staircase leading up to the clock shop. He just wasn't interested in this discussion right now. Right now, the worry of his heart spoke louder than the logic of his mind.

Bishop approached with a rare humility Sir Alfred had seen only once before. He bowed his head as a sign of respect and placed one hand on the shoulder of Sir Alfred's tweed blazer. "Friend, I am aware that patience is a virtue I have yet to master."

Sir Alfred waited for Bishop to slowly tilt up his head and locked eyes with him to offer in return his own sign of respect.

Bishop continued, "But I possess other virtues which have served the Society well for a great many years. Tenacity. Loyalty."

Sir Alfred nodded.

Bishop went on, "With you and Freemont as my witnesses, I pricked my finger and spilled my blood into the Keepers' Urn, swearing my oath..." his voice cracked, "...On the souls of the family I chose to forgo having, that I would stop at nothing to protect time."

Sir Alfred could not deny the truth of Bishop's words and the honor of his intentions. He waited patiently for Bishop to finish.

"And now time – is in great danger. If Gabriel gets hold of the Sacred Object before we do, he will surely make good on his promise of so many years ago...declare himself the Father and rule supremely over all dimensions of space and time."

The thought of it sent a chill through Sir Alfred that nearly buckled his knees.

Bishop continued, "So please, brother. Do not ask me to merely sit and wait. For I fear it may be too difficult a command to obey."

Sir Alfred took a deep sigh. He hadn't heard such heartfelt words from Bishop in many years. "What are you proposing, old friend?"

"In the event that Gabriel should break Freemont before Julian and his friends are able to help – then you and I are left as the sole protectors of the Sacred Object. And we certainly can't protect something if we don't know where, or even *what*, it is." Bishop looked at Sir Alfred plainly. "We have to search for it. We have to look in every crack and cranny of this clock shop."

Sir Alfred shook his head immediately. "No, Bishop. That does not sit well with me. It's insubordinate."

Bishop urged, "Think about it. We are all alone here now. In the home of our Senior Keeper, with the freedom to properly search every inch of this space for the answer to the riddle of the Sacred Object – a riddle we've pondered our entire lives!"

"But there are risks, Bishop. There are reasons that only one man has been trusted with the Sacred Object. It can be dangerous to be so close to such power." For the first time in as long as he could recall, Sir Alfred raised his voice at Bishop, "We were not *meant* to know!" The echo of his words bounced around in the cellar and came back at him from every side. Immediately he regretted it, but he did expect Bishop got the message.

That is, until Bishop spoke again. "Not meant to know?" Bishop repeated, "Do you know who you sound like?"

Sir Alfred knew exactly whom Bishop was referring to. Freemont always did things by the book. He never wanted to bend the rules merely to suit his own personal needs, or even the needs of the Society, not even if it were for a greater good.

In fact, many of the Keepers criticized that it was Freemont's unwillingness to bend the rules so many years ago to let Gabriel into the Elders' circle that led to the young Keeper's uprising and, eventually...the Second Great Battle.

"There are many who would take that comparison as a very high compliment," Sir Alfred responded.

"And on any other day, it would be. But not this one, I'm afraid. Abiding by ancient rules when faced with modern problems is not the sign of a leader." Bishop pulled from Sir Alfred's front blazer pocket the bible and held it under the harsh glow of the light bulb overhead. "This bible doesn't have a chapter on what to do when you're about to lose everything because it assumes that Good will always defeat Evil."

Sir Alfred answered, "Hasn't it?"

Bishop dropped the book to the floor, kicking up a cloud of dust that separated them like a wall. "I don't know, Sir Alfred. Why don't you ask Julian's mum and dad that question? Or our frozen friend back down in the Keepers' Chamber?"

Sir Alfred's eyes closed slowly. It was a punch in the gut that left him breathless. Bishop was right. It was Evil who had orphaned Julian. And that same Evil who put their kind-hearted mate, Linus, in a catatonic state, forgotten by time. Sir Alfred pushed up his glasses to wipe away a tear that tried desperately to hide in the corner of his eye.

Bishop went on, "It took only one night to discover this rift, Sir Alfred. Imagine what else we might find with our newfound freedom to search."

Sir Alfred gently turned toward Bishop and acquiesced with a nod.

Bishop nodded back. "Okay, then. Let us get to work. For if we find the Sacred Object before Gabriel does, there is nothing he can do to hurt time."

For what seemed hours, the two old friends scoured Freemont's apartment above the shop, searching for anything – any sign of the Sacred Object. Still, they found nothing.

Petey sniffed under beds, thrashed at pillow covers and tumbled inside the clothes hamper, to Sir Alfred's chagrin.

"Can you get that infernal creature to behave?" he snapped then turned toward Bishop. "What is it with you and that ferret, anyway?"

"I've told you a hundred times. All great men have great pets."

Sir Alfred immediately wished he hadn't opened that Pandora's Box again.

But it was too late. Bishop was already off with it. "And the truth is that they owe their greatness to their pets. Ptolemy II, King of Egypt, kept a white bear in captivity, but methinks it wasn't a polar bear at all. It was an albino, just like Petey."

Petey scurried across the floor, sniffing at everything. Bishop followed him.

"Then there was the Roman Emperor, Nero, who was said to love only one creature in his life - his pet tigress, Phoebe."

Sir Alfred watched Bishop unclasp a gold chain from around his neck and settle it in the air.

"What are you doing?" Sir Alfred asked.

"Something I should have done hours ago. Something Freemont would have done." Bishop pinched a charm that dangled from the chain, previously hidden under his pinstripe shirt and vest, a charm of the minute hand of a clock.

Sir Alfred watched intensely.

Bishop dangled the charm over a flame from a candle. It began to twirl very slowly. He spoke to it in rhyme.

"Any friend of time is a friend of mine.
But now you are much more.
Search this room for what is oldest here.
And point me to its core."

Petey popped his head from the clothes hamper and stared as the charm continued to twirl, faster and faster. Suddenly, it stopped so abruptly that it trembled.

It was pointing right at Freemont's closet.

Bishop looked at Sir Alfred and smiled. "Come to papa." Slowly, Bishop stepped into the closet. The charm pointed straight down, at the worn carpeted floor.

Bishop lifted the carpet. Under it, was a small handle to a compartment. He turned to his old friend, who nodded. In seconds they would discover the Sacred Object, they were sure of it. This was a time to be extremely careful.

Gently, Bishop pulled the small compartment door open and revealed Freemont's Senior Keeper's gown.

Sir Alfred's voice came from behind him with a disappointed sigh, "That's enough, Bishop."

Bishop stared at the gown, thinking. His shoulders slumped. This was an object, all right, but it surely wasn't the one he had been hoping for.

Sir Alfred put a kind hand on his friend's shoulder. "Let's have a cup of tea, Bishop. That will clear our thoughts."

Petey scampered ahead of the two men, racing underfoot mischievously.

"Blast that annoying rodent!" Sir Alfred growled, as he sidestepped the creature on his way down the stairs back to the clock shop. "One of these days, he'll be the death of me!"

Bishop resumed from where he had left off, listing all his examples of great pets throughout time, "And arguably the greatest Pharaoh of all times, Ramses II, kept a male lion as his trusty sidekick, not only in his palace but also with him on the battlefield."

At that moment, Sir Alfred tripped over Petey and fell headlong in what seemed like very slow motion.

"Sir Alfred!" Bishop looked on, terrified.

Sir Alfred's lanky frame landed at the bottom of the stairs with quite a thud.

For a moment, all the clocks tick-tocked extra loud and pendulums swayed wildly.

Then Sir Alfred noticed something truly awful. The giant 24-Hour Glass had been shaken off its delicate balance. Sir Alfred approached it worriedly, his hands outstretched.

The massive glass structure teetered on the uneven wooden floor planks. It swayed ominously, and then came crashing down - straight at him.

"NO!" Bishop called out from behind, leaping to move his friend from harm's way.

The 24-Hour Glass smashed on the floor, spilling millions of grains of sand like water from a broken dam.

Both men sat up against Freemont's front room display case and stared at the wreck that was the clock. But it wasn't all the sand that drew their attention. It was the tiny glass bottle hidden within it, apparently having been disguised in the frame of the hourglass. Slowly, it rolled over the grainy sand on the floor, to them.

"Freemont. You old devil," murmured Sir Alfred, as he picked up the bottle and carefully withdrew the note inside it. He unrolled the delicate paper gingerly to reveal an ancient and very beautiful portrait.

The brush strokes in the tiny painting were fine and meticulous, depicting an old man with long, white hair and a flowing white beard. He wore a crown of leaves, a long gown, and a medallion bearing the Keeper's insignia. He also cradled a sleeping baby.

Bishop uttered with reverence, "It's the Father, isn't it?"

Sir Alfred nodded, "Most definitely."

"And the child?" asked Bishop.

Sir Alfred gently passed his fingertips over the magnificent, vivid portrait, feeling each brush stroke as if he were reading Braille. "Baby New Year, I presume," he said. "It represents the passing of time, from old to new."

Bishop had to wonder aloud, "But why would Freemont hide it?"

Silence fell as the two men pondered the mystery of the tiny note. Suddenly, both were rudely startled from their thoughts by the sound of a loud jangle and a heavy thump from the cellar.

Someone had just joined them.

"Who could it be?" Bishop asked, trying to seem brave.

"We have to find out."

They cautiously stepped on the bottom stair to unhinge the mechanism that would expose the secret stairs going down to the cellar. Bishop peered down into the cellar cautiously. All seemed quiet save for the humming of the rift.

With a sigh, they began to retreat from the hidden entrance when suddenly, quite out of nowhere, a creature the size of a large dog crawled out of the cellar, panicked, and clambered out a very high and very dim window, and out of sight!

The two men shared a look of shock.

"Was that a...wombat?" Bishop puzzled.

FIFTEEN

The Forest Fairy

Julian, Lily and Martin listened as closely as they could to the echoes and whispers that seemed to come from another time and place.

"Look at you now, old man," said a disembodied Gabriel.

All three friends exchanged a look of dread.

Then, suddenly, Julian heard something he'd been missing for what seemed years. The soft, familiar voice of his granddad.

"No, look at you, Gabriel. You were smart enough to create a machine that could penetrate all dimensions of time, but too impatient to even learn how to properly fly it."

Gabriel began to respond, but the echoing whispers from the past receded, then faded away completely.

"That conversation wasn't finished," Lily observed.

Julian scratched his head with Granddad's cane, perplexed.

Something caught Lily's eye. "The cane," she said. "There's something about that cane. You waved it into the cave when you were screaming..."

Martin finished her thought, "...And the echoes that came back were from another time..."

Julian looked down at Granddad's antique cane and recalled yet again a conversation they had once had.

Between this cane and me, one of us is as old as time itself, Julian.

Julian's eyes grew large, "I think this cane may have once belonged to the Father."

Lily asked, "The Father?"

"Father Time. I think this was his cane!" Julian said excitedly.

Martin sat down on a rock and wiped his face with his hand. "Jules, maybe you were right. Maybe we need to rest."

Julian insisted, "No. I'm serious. I think it was Father Time's cane and it was passed down through the Keepers to my granddad. I think it's...magical."

Lily lit up at the prospect of it. "Try it again!" she implored him.

"How?" Julian asked.

"Just say something to create another echo. Anything. And wave it around like last time at the wall."

"What shall I say?" Julian asked.

"Anything, Jules," said Martin. "First thing that comes to mind."

"I feel stupid," Julian said, embarrassed. Julian looked away from Lily's expectant eyes and back at Martin.

"Just give it a try, Julian. We don't have anything to lose." For the first time in a long while, Martin smiled encouragingly at Julian.

Closing his eyes in expectation, Julian whirled Granddad's cane in the air in a side-to-side figure-eight pattern.

Nothing.

"Try it again." Lily smiled with encouragement.

Julian waved the cane around in the air again, this time reciting the old man's favorite rhyme, the one he'd greeted countless customers with for as long as he'd owned the store.

"Welcome to the AM/PM Emp-or-ee-um.
My own personal time museum.
If it's a clock you seek, look around and see 'em.
Or tell me your wish, and I'll make it be 'um."

There was a slight humming sound, a static-like crackle, and then…the evil voice picked up from where it had left off as if nothing had happened. "You'd better watch who you insult, old fool. You're in my world now, and you'll do as I say."

Freemont's voice returned, aged but strong. "I will never help you, Gabriel. Look into your heart. You know it to be true."

"Truth is a matter of perspective," Gabriel argued. "Right now, the only truth I know is that if you don't give me what I need by the time we reach my lair, I am going to treat you to a dip…"

The three friends looked at each other, horrified.

Gabriel's voice burned with the sizzling heat of molten lava, "…In the Lakes of Fire."

The echoes disappeared again, leaving nothing but silence.

Lily scratched her head. "The conversation we just heard. It must have happened right here. But earlier?"

Martin considered the notion. "Yes, of course. Your grandfather and this Gabriel bloke must have walked past this very cave, Julian. We are on their trail after all!"

Julian nodded in agreement, trying to appear encouraged.

"We must get to these Lakes of Fire before they do," Martin concluded. "No waiting until morning, Julian. We must continue on right now!"

Julian knew he was right. He stared out the cavern, up at the starry sky still aglow from its orbiting purple moons. He thought to himself, *Morning must be just moments away. It won't be too bad, right?*

Suddenly, Julian heard another voice in his mind; only this one was higher-pitched and beautiful, like the song of a delicate bird. *Strangers must be announced.*

Julian knew his friends would think he was crazy. "Who said that?" He stepped out of the cave, searching. Were the echoing voices back?

Martin looked at Lily, "Who is he talking to? Where's he going?"

Up ahead, Julian saw something odd. A faintly glowing silhouette. He crept closer.

Stop and announce yourself.

With a sharp intake of breath, Julian realized that the owner of the tiny voice was a small fairy, half his size, hovering just feet away.

Her voice and shape in the cascading moonlight were mesmerizing. With a soft hum of wings, the fairy flittered closer and gestured firmly to Julian.

Julian's eyes traced the fairy's details in wonder. Large gossamer wings, each thrice the size of her porcelain face, beat softly. A white tunic was draped around her doll-like form. Her head was teardrop in shape with golden braids of hair that coiled at the top like a turban. The fairy's large, gentle green eyes reminded Julian of a photo Granddad once showed him of his own mum. An image burned forever into his memory.

All strangers must be announced, the voice in his head repeated. The fairy looked at Julian strangely, as if he'd grown a second nose.

"Julian!" cautioned Lily.

But the fairy and her flowing white robe seemingly hypnotized Julian. She was such a stark contrast to the darkness around her.

"Why?" Julian asked the fairy.

Martin and Lily approached cautiously and flanked Julian on both sides. His own private army.

There was no answer from the fairy, only curious eyes that scanned him up and down.

"What is this place? Where am I?" Julian pressed.

Martin spoke instead, "She obviously isn't going to answer our questions, Jules. Probably doesn't even understand what you're saying."

Suddenly, without opening her mouth, the fairy responded with a single word that played in Julian's mind like a song. *Delphisola.*

Julian nodded. It was the same name that the ladybug, or lady beetle, rather, had given him. "What is your name?" he asked.

Florinia, the voice returned in his head.

"That's very pretty," answered Julian.

Martin and Lily shared puzzled looks. *What is very pretty?* Was their friend going mad?

Julian felt their stares and turned to them, "She just spoke to us. Did you not hear? Her name is Florinia. She, too, called this place...Delphisola."

Suddenly impatient, the fairy zoomed up to Julian and glared at him. *You must come with me.*

Julian moved back from the fairy a few steps. "What? Where?"

The fairy came close again. Suddenly, her face changed from annoyance to a great, consuming interest.

Lily and Martin exchanged a concerned look.

The fairy's thoughts again were heard in Julian's mind. *You smell different. You look different.*

"Thanks," Julian answered somewhat sarcastically.

Are – are you The One?

Julian stumbled, "The who?"

The Savior.

"The Savior?" Julian again backed up a step. What in the heck was this fairy going on about?

Her aura began to glow more brightly. *You are! You are The One! It was foretold!*

Julian cried out, "No, I am Julian. Julian Rigby."

"What's she saying now, Julian?" Lily curiously prodded.

"She wants to know if I'm her savior."

Lily was visibly disturbed by this conversation. As much as she loved meeting a real, live fairy, this is not how she envisioned it might go. "I don't trust anything that will only speak with one of us, Julian. We are a team." She turned toward the fairy and waved her away like a pesky housefly. "Shoo!"

The fairy retreated, falling into the soil before rolling back up gracefully. Despite the fall, her silken white tunic remained unsoiled. She shifted her eyes to lock with Lily's. *The prophecy tells of the Savior who will come to restore the light we lost when the Dark One arrived and cracked our world.*

"The Dark One?" Lily asked, "Do you mean Gabriel?"

Martin threw his hands in the air, "Great. Now she's speaking to you, too?"

The fairy fluttered her large wings more quickly and glided back to Julian. *Are you or are you not the man the prophecy speaks of?*

Martin tried to intervene, "Can we just have a normal conversation here? Is that so much to ask?"

Julian shook his head. "I'm sorry, but I'm not a man at all. I am a boy," he answered.

The soft, white glow emanating from the delicate creature's figure dimmed. She flitted around him a few more times, confused and conflicted. She again inspected his scent, his aura and his character.

With sadness, she stated once more: *All strangers must be announced.* She remained suspended in the air for a long moment, then as quickly as she arrived, she darted away, across an open field and into the dense forest that lay beyond it.

"Wait!" Julian shouted.

"Let her go, Julian," Lily pleaded.

But he could not. Julian ran toward the dark forest after the fairy as if he were helplessly connected to her by a gossamer thread.

"Julian!" Martin watched his friend, still confused.

Julian was quickly fading from view following the faint glow of the fairy.

Lily looked at Martin and shrugged. "We are a team."

The two friends set off into the dusky violet evening after their quickly disappearing friend.

SIXTEEN

Detective Riley Returns

Sir Alfred and Bishop stared out the window to where the mysterious wombat had escaped. Suddenly, the chime over the clock shop's front door jingled, startling them yet again.
Who on earth had entered the clock shop so boldly? Surely it couldn't be Gabriel again?

Slowly, the two men carefully and inconspicuously closed the secret stairway and tucked away the tiny and mysterious portrait of Father Time, then turned back to the front of the shop.

"Tea sounds terrif, thanks for offering," said Detective Riley as he leaned on the counter and beamed at a startled Sir Alfred.

Bishop picked up Petey and set him on his shoulder, "Sorry, we're closed."

Detective Riley looked past the broken hourglass at the otherwise recently reorganized clock shop. He saw nothing of the destruction from the last time he was there for Julian's arrest.

"What happened?" he couldn't help asking.

"We're finishing up cleaning," answered Sir Alfred, wondering why the detective had returned.

"You cleaned my crime scene?"

Suddenly, a succession of screeching tires was heard outside the front door, followed by the loud sound of car doors opening and closing.

"Crime scene? You called it a missing persons case the other day after jailing a twelve-year-old for vandalizing his own home," Bishop snipped.

Detective Riley narrowed his eyes at Bishop. It was clear that these two would rather have a fistfight than continue any conversation. "Things have changed."

Calmly, Sir Alfred stepped between them. "This is understandable, Detective. However, you did not cordon off the store or give any instructions to stay away, so how could we have known? Besides, I'm Julian's guardian on behalf of Freemont, and I felt it best to return his home to as 'normal' a state as it could be."

Detective Riley looked at Sir Alfred, thinking over his perfectly logical argument when, suddenly, the shuffling, chattering sound of a crowd of men grew outside the shop door. "Where is the boy?" Detective Riley began to look around. "I need to ask him more questions."

Bishop stepped in front of the detective's path to block him from moving any farther. "Not here."

"Yes, Mr. Bishop. I can see that. Would you care to elaborate?"

"No."

"Julian is with his friends and I'm not quite sure when he will return," said Sir Alfred.

Detective Riley snorted, despite himself. "Well now. Some guardian you've turned out to be. I'm sure Mr. Freemont Rigby will be mighty grateful for how well you are taking care of his ward."

From the corner of his eye, Sir Alfred spied something strange... an otherworldly chameleon was creeping out of a crack from the secret cellar stairs. He desperately tried to tell Bishop – using only his eyes - *The stairs aren't closed!*

Calmly and intentionally, Bishop took a seat on the last stair to lock it shut for good.

Sir Alfred maintained his cool and straightened his vest. "So, if there's nothing else, I'll show you to the door, Detective."

But Detective Riley wasn't quite ready to go. He slid a crisp, white sheet of paper onto the front counter. On it, was embossed the Westminster Court seal of approval. "This, gentlemen, is a warrant." Riley smiled and leaned on the counter confidently.

The chameleon streaked up the wall and clung directly atop the unsuspecting detective.

Eyes bulging with worry and anger, Bishop asked, "What kind of warrant?"

"The searching kind." Detective Riley couldn't have been more pleased. He turned toward the front door, clapped his hands and smiled.

Instantly, the door of the shop burst open to reveal ten officers, waiting on his command.

"Let's move, gents. I want every detail of this place inspected."

"Yes, sir!" The men set off in all directions like cockroaches. Frightened, the strange chameleon leapt out the window.

Bishop shot a worried look at Sir Alfred but received only a shrug in return.

Detective Riley accompanied his men toward the back of the shop, stopped, and turned back to Sir Alfred and Bishop. "Mr. Bishop, would you be a dear and fetch me that cup of tea? Then, you and Mr. Alfred have a seat somewhere comfortable – where I can keep an eye on you."

Bishop gritted his teeth and did as he was told, heading toward the kitchen.

The enthusiastic officers poured into the shop and began to scour every inch of it while

Bishop bitterly fired up the flame on the stove and clanged a kettle on top.

Petey, perched on his shoulder, squeaked in his ear.

"Don't you worry, Petey. These simpletons couldn't find their own reflection in a mirror."

Sir Alfred glared at Bishop, then lit his pipe and did his best to appear relaxed, puffing a cloud of smoke that lingered in the air. Playfully, he drew a circle with his finger that stretched the smoke into the shape of a clock that ticked as a reminder of their mission at hand. He admired his little creation until it slowly disappeared.

Bishop wasn't so charmed. "We'll never find the Sacred Object with all these idiots rummaging through the place," he whispered nervously to Sir Alfred.

Sir Alfred answered back under his breath, "Right now, I'm more concerned with them finding something than I am with us *not* finding something, Bishop."

The teakettle whistle began to shriek.

Detective Riley appeared in the kitchen suddenly. "Black," he spouted.

"Beg your pardon?" Sir Alfred returned.

"Make mine a black tea. Darjeeling if you have it. If not, improvise." Before Bishop could respond, Detective Riley turned back to his men.

"Check under the rugs. Dust those shelves for prints. Chop-chop now. A fellow doesn't just disappear into thin air." He returned to Sir Alfred and Bishop with a knowing smile, "Does he, now?"

The teakettle whistled insistently. Bishop glared at Riley, then reached into the cupboard to find a teacup for his new nemesis. No luck. Then, he stepped up onto his toes and found one tucked into the corner.

It was a familiar handmade cup finger-painted with the words, 'World's Greatest Granddad.' Freemont's personal favorite. The one he'd never offered to the 'Bridge Club' for as long as they'd known him.

The memory of Freemont was filling Bishop's heart with pain, when suddenly something in the cup caught his eye.

The water poured from the kettle into the cup had magnified a tiny inscription hidden on the inside bottom. Bishop peered closer for a better look.

Sir Alfred looked at Bishop, wondering if his old friend needed to sit down, perhaps. "What is it, Bishop?"

At the bottom of the cup, a series of numbers warped and wiggled as the water struggled to settle.

"That my tea, Mr. Bishop?" Riley re-entered the kitchen and reached for the mug.

Bishop snatched it away, "No, it's not."

Detective Riley stared, nonplussed for the first time.

"This one is mine. Green tea, not black," Bishop added, clutching the cup tightly.

Detective Riley furrowed his brow. "Green? And you fancy yourself a Brit?"

Bishop forced a smile and took an extra slurpy sip of the hot water, pretending to love it.

Riley stared at him for a moment, then glowered and returned to his searching men.

Watching Riley carefully, Bishop promptly slid the cup across the table to Sir Alfred, who peered into it, then reached deep into his blazer pocket for his small copy of the Keepers' Bible and flipped open its back cover.

"Let's see." Sir Alfred began to scribble quickly, as he jotted down the numbers exactly as they appeared in the cup. 13:32, 23:10, 4:40, 16:03, 3:58, 2:22, 1:19, 17:55, 23:10.

Bishop whispered excitedly, "They are times. Times of day. I am sure of it."

Sir Alfred shook his head softly, "You, my friend, are surely wrong."

A few officers walked through the room, carrying some of Freemont's possessions. One had a lamp, the other a hairbrush.

Bishop looked at his old friend, "How do you figure I'm wrong?"

"Well, you may know science, but I know the Keepers' Bible. And these, Bishop, are most definitely not times of day. They are verses." To prove his point, Sir Alfred flipped through the little book and landed at the first coordinate: Chapter thirteen, verse thirty-two. He read quietly so only Bishop could hear. "*Of concerning that day or that hour, no one knows, not even the angels in Heaven, nor the Son, but only…the Father.*"

Bishop crinkled his nose. He never understood the prophecies of men nearly as much as the formulas of mathematics. "You expect me to remember stuff like that? Or even understand it?" he responded defensively.

Sir Alfred puzzled over it as well. "I don't think it's the *meaning* we are supposed to take note of, Bishop."

Bishop shrugged, "I don't follow."

"Come now, Bishop. For all your mathematical brilliance, you don't recall as junior members in the Society our most basic set of codes?"

Suddenly it hit Bishop. "IWP!" he blurted out.

"Shh. Yes, Initial Word Phrasing. Take the first word of every sentence to form a new one."

Sir Alfred examined the first word of the verse they had just read. "Of," he said aloud.

Bishop scrambled for a napkin and a pen as Sir Alfred flipped determinedly through the pages, reading each and every verse that the coordinates called for.

Finally, they reached the last set. Chapter twenty-three, verse ten. "*All knew that when the fullness of time had come, He sent forth his Son, born of woman, born by Law.*"

A few more officers passed through the kitchen. Sir Alfred pretended to be casually reading his book, disguising his face as he called out the last word in IWP code to his cohort. "All," he said, inconspicuously.

Bishop scribbled this last word on the napkin, but the phrase he had written did not make sense.

Of tick makes us what sacred is most all.

He looked up at Sir Alfred, beaming. "Wait. It's scrambled. Wait. I know it. *What makes us tick is most sacred of all,*" he proudly read the decoded phrase aloud.

Sir Alfred immediately lit up with a smile of his own. "Nicely done, Bishop." He closed his Keepers' Bible and immediately tore up the napkin. Then, he intentionally knocked the teacup off the table, shattering it to pieces against the kitchen floor.

Detective Riley and his officers rushed into the room. "What was that?" Riley demanded to know.

"Oops, it appears that I am bit clumsy today," Sir Alfred feigned.

Detective Riley paused, skeptically surveying the room.

Awkwardly, Sir Alfred tried to sweep up the shattered cup pieces with his shoe.

"What is it with you two and tea?" Riley knelt down and examined the little broken pieces carefully.

Sir Alfred and Bishop watched with bated breath, but Riley didn't seem to notice anything unusual. "Walker, have someone clean this up. And then post a man in here with these two."

Sir Alfred and Bishop exchanged a look. How were they to continue piecing this mysterious puzzle together so they could help Julian as quickly as possible, with Riley interfering?

Just then, they heard a frightened shout and the sound of scuffling. "Sir! Detective Riley!" The shouts grew louder.

Sir Alfred and Bishop's eyes widened. The officers had discovered the secret cellar stairs and were going down there now!

Bishop immediately snapped his fingers as he'd done earlier for Julian, producing the same silvery ripple. He was about hide under another blanket of air pulled around himself and Sir Alfred when Riley grabbed him forcefully by the shoulder.

"You two. Come with me."

What greeted Sir Alfred and Bishop at the bottom of the stairs was the worst sight imaginable. An officer was already halfway through the rift, and getting stretched like toffee as he struggled against its powerful pull. Only his legs were still visible.

"Don't just stand there! Help him!" Detective Riley commanded the other officers, who stood by dumbfounded.

Four officers grasped the legs of their unfortunate companion as the rift pulsed and crackled more loudly than before. As strong as they were, the officers were no match for the pull of the rift. With a sucking sound, the bobby was drawn in and slurped up like so much linguini.

Riley stared, mouth agape. Then, as if in slow motion, he turned to Officer Walker, who stood rooted to the spot. He took the officer's handcuffs and chained Bishop and Sir Alfred together. "Someone get me the Prime Minister on the line. Now!"

SEVENTEEN

A Disenchanted Forest

Julian chased after the Forest Fairy as if he had a chance to catch her, but she simply glided too swiftly across the landscape.

He noticed that, curiously, the dainty fairy never actually took flight. Despite her large, feathery wings, she merely skimmed over the ground, touching down only as often as necessary to propel herself forward. The fairy reminded Julian of a graceful but flightless bird that yearned to soar but was never quite able to.

Yet without full flight, the fairy outpaced him. While Julian slowed down, huffing and puffing from exertion, the fairy continued on until she disappeared into the darkness of the trees ahead.

Julian leaned against Granddad's cane and shouted one final plea to her, "I need your help, fairy!"

There was no response. No mind message this time.

Exasperated and discouraged, Julian looked up at the purple crescent moons above and the full golden moon they orbited. He wondered why they still shone so brightly. “Go away! Where is your sun? Your dawn?” he shouted at the moons like a frustrated interrogator.

A black shadow flitted against the moons. Julian stared in wonder as he saw that it was a large crow, circling above him. Could it possibly be the same black crow he saw after the seaweed saved him from the waterfall?

He directed his anger toward the crow. “Do you follow me, bird? Are you a scavenger? Well, I’m sorry to disappoint you, but I’m not dead yet.” He did shoo away the crow this time, hoping that his bad luck would fly away too.

“Who are you talking to now, Julian?”

Julian turned back to see his friends, now just ten feet away. Martin was looking at him quizzically.

“She went in there,” Julian said helplessly as he pointed ahead at the dark forest.

Together, they stared at the forest. It seemed too thick to allow in even the smallest amount of light from either the amber or purple moons.

Julian shook his head, cursing this endless night. “If only the sun would rise...”

Lily followed, "But who knows when that will be? We have no choice."

Martin puffed his chest once again. "We must go after her," he declared.

Lily turned to Julian noticing something wasn't right. "Julian, are you getting shorter?"

Julian looked down at his feet. Come to think of it, he had been feeling a slight sinking sensation in the last few moments. He thought it was the familiar sensation of frustration he was getting all too used to.

Martin shouted, "Jules, you're sinking!"

Martin was right. Julian was already ankle deep in what looked like glass marbles of swirling colors too hard to make out in the moonlight. What was certain was that the marbles, or stones, or whatever they were, were starting to pick up speed as they sucked Julian downward.

Lily strained her eyes to get a better look. She stepped closer, but only to the edge of the rock bed. She puzzled, "Quick...stone?"

Julian sank another few inches into the colored glass stones that churned around his legs like the teeth of a monster trying to gobble him up.

"Julian – quick!" Martin was reaching toward him.

As hard as he might try, Julian couldn't reach Martin's outstretched hand. Then he had an idea. He reached toward Martin with the cane. But Martin still couldn't reach him.

Julian sank more, this time to his knees. Lily caught the moonlight shine off his belt buckle and remembered its use. "Julian, your belt!"

That's right, he thought. *I'll use my Heavy-Duty Tow Belt!* Julian tucked Granddad's cane under his armpit and unclasped the two loops of wire from inside his belt buckle – the spot once covered by the buck knife portion of the Rigby Knuckle. He pulled on the two wire cables from around a tiny pulley until they were long enough to toss to Lily and Martin. "Fix the clasps to your own buckles and stand firm. There's a mechanism inside the clasp that will retract the cables and tow me out to you."

Lily and Martin did as they were told but Julian continued to sink even more. Now up to his thighs, he began to panic. *This gadget was only a prototype after all*, he remembered with fear. "Hold still," he instructed. "Three, two, one." He flipped the switch and immediately it did start to pull…it pulled Martin and Lily toward the pit!

"Julian!" Lily struggled to detach the cable.

Try as they might not to wind up in Julian's predicament, Lily and Martin were soon themselves neck deep in the swirling stones.

Julian waved the cane wildly in the air. "Forest fairy! Do something! Somebody do something! QUICK!"

Suddenly, something did happen. The quickstone...quickened! They all felt it. It was as if, somehow, they had been shifted into fast forward.

Lily realized immediately what had happened. "The cane. It's making the quickstone go quicker!" Lily managed to get out that much before the stones began to cover her chin.

Martin spit out a few glowing stones from his mouth and shouted, "If it can go faster, then it can go slower!"

Clatter. Slither.

Martin was now lost within the stones.

"Julian!" screamed Lily before she also disappeared before his eyes.

Julian couldn't believe what was happening. It was as awful as any nightmare he'd ever had. Alone in a world dipped in black. The sight of losing the only two friends he had ever known overwhelmed his heart.

He exploded with emotion. "Back you go! Back in time!" He waved Granddad's cane frantically as the churning stones reached his lips, kept rising, and covered his eyes and then...Julian was gone.

Total silence, save for the rustle of a wave of stones that rippled in the pit. Even the whispers that had skimmed through the grass held their collective breath.

The shadow of the black crow appeared over the stones, signaling the return of the bird that seemed so fascinated by their journey. Suddenly...

The ripple of the wave in the stones began again, only this time in reverse. The swirling stones picked up speed and Julian began to reappear – time was moving backward!

The nightmare reversed itself until all three friends were ejected and returned as safe and as sound as they had been before it all had begun. Not a single scratch was found on any of them. It was like it had never happened.

Martin, Lily and Julian were stunned. They stared at Granddad's cane, amazed by its awesome time-bending powers.

"You were saying, Julian, that it belonged to...the Father?" Lily asked.

"May I touch it?" Martin reached for the cane.

Julian lifted it toward Martin for a touch.

They inspected it closely, completely mesmerized.

Finally, a smile returned to Lily's golden face, crinkling her almond eyes joyfully. Perhaps this adventure was destined to deliver all she hoped for after all. "Father Time's cane!" she laughed.

Julian's face brightened. She was right. And he'd had it the entire time. There was no time to waste now. Julian pointed toward the forest, "Shall we?"

Lily and Martin nodded, still a bit shaken, but it wasn't long before the three friends were making their way toward the great, dark forest ahead.

Soon, they were standing at the edge of the forbidding tree line.

"Maybe you're right, Martin. Maybe following the Forest Fairy is a stupid idea." Julian turned to his friends, trying not to show how intimidated he was by what lay ahead.

"Nonsense, Jules. You were right. She is the only chance we have of finding these so-called Lakes of Fire and getting to your granddad."

Julian nodded unconvincingly. It was clear that Martin's confidence in him had grown exponentially. He only wished that he shared the sentiment.

The three of them huddled close together and stepped slowly into the forest. The thick cover of trees blocked out the pale moonlight almost completely. What little the friends could see were just shades and shapes of varying degrees of dark. Leaves, bushes, branches and rocks under the cover of infinite nightfall. Martin stepped on a twig that snapped loudly.

"Shh. Listen," Julian implored. In the distance, a strange sound undulated like waves of water.

"Is that...crying?" questioned Lily.

"I don't know." Julian looked at his friends inquisitively.

"One way to find out," said Martin.

Together, they followed the whimpering sound deeper and deeper into the forest. Slowly, the whimpers gave way to sobs. The friends were completely mystified. Who – or what – was crying?

Gloop! Splash!

Head to toe, Lily was covered in what appeared to be tree sap. "Argh!" she shouted. "What is this?"

No answer, only another undignified sap splash.

"Lily, move out of the way!" Martin succeeded in shoving her out of the way, only to get covered with sap himself.

But Lily wasn't concerned with the sap. She was peering up into the tree, looking both curious and moved. Then her mouth fell open with astonishment.

"What is it, Lily?" Julian asked nervously. "What do you see?"

Lily didn't hear him. "Is it you who sobs?" she seemed to be addressing the tree itself.

Martin and Julian exchanged a worried look. What was up there?

Suddenly, a voice boomed back down, "Do not mind me, little one."

"I don't mind," said Lily to the wispy auburn leaves of the massive, old Weeping Willow that towered over her like an ancient umbrella.

Julian leaned in, curiously. He saw now what she saw...a tired face in those wispy leaves. It was a face with long, droopy eyes and overgrown hair. It sobbed again, then down came another gallon of tear sap.

Lily moved easily out of its way.

Splash!

"Forgive my tears that wet your feet. I cannot keep them from falling any more," the booming voice said.

"But why do you weep, Willow?" Lily inquired.

The rugged voice continued to cry ever more. "It is all I can do, as I have lost my identity and live without purpose. A mere fossil of the

Enchanted Forest. A statue in time." More tears fell from above, forcing the friends to shuffle and dodge as if they were playing some strange schoolyard game.

Leaping to avoid another punishing soak, Lily called back up to the tree, "Did you say Enchanted Forest?"

Julian could see how the name tickled Lily's fancy. But more than that, it was evident that she was genuinely concerned for this somber creature, stuck in a state of grief.

The tree, lost in its sorrow, did not reply.

Lily tried again. "Forgive us, we did not mean to frighten you," apologized Lily.

The tree chuckled, cheered just slightly by the notion. "You did not frighten me, little one. I knew you were coming."

The three children all paused.

"How did you know?" Julian asked.

"Our root system is much more complicated than you might think. It connects us to all living things in the forest, and even some just outside the forest's edge, like the Gossiping Grass."

Martin chewed on those words, "Gossiping Grass? Wait a tick! You mean the whispers that we heard coming down the hill? In the grass? I knew I wasn't crazy!"

The tree continued, "They told us of a creature who called himself...*boy*. You are the boys?"

Lily put a finger in the air, "Well, technically..."

Suddenly there was another booming sob, only this time it was female in tone. It surprised them from the other side, "Oh, look Bogford. Now you've got me started, too."

The male voice answered back gently, "I am so sorry, my dearest Mergda. I do so hate it when you cry."

Mergda continued, "We were once so useful. It was the Willows who gave shade to all travelers of the forest. Shade from our bountiful three suns."

Bogford added, "We were once guardians of the forest, trusted and honored. But when the Dark One came, everything changed. We are but statues now, forgotten by time. Who needs shade when there are no more suns?"

Julian stiffened, "No suns? You mean...morning is not going to come?" Julian tried to keep the panic out of his voice. How much longer could he ignore his fcar of the darkness?

Mergda answered, "Morning hasn't come for an eternity on Delphisola. When the Dark One pierced our world, time stopped forever. If you doubt me, just have a look in my leaves." The tree lifted a heavy branch to reveal thousands of tiny, crystalline cocoons, frozen in time.

The friends gasped at the sad sight and, for the first time, saw that all of the trees had cocoons permanently attached to them like a ghost forest of butterflies never to be.

The gloomy revelation stirred Julian to action. "We need to find the Dark One," Julian declared firmly.

His friends looked at him with renewed admiration. "Do you know where the Lakes of Fire are?" he asked.

The trees seemed to groan and sigh before Bogford answered. "I cannot speak to the location of the Lakes of Fire, but I can tell you that it is an archipelago of volcanoes. The largest holds his lair."

"An archipelago of volcanoes?" Julian studied the forest around him. Suddenly everything felt alive. An eye blinked in a shadow he had not noticed before. A bush shook as if it harbored some creature watching them. *If grass can talk, what else is possible in this Enchanted Forest?* he wondered.

"Do you know which direction we should take?" asked Lily.

"Or how to find the Forest Fairy we chased into here?" Martin chimed in.

With a gentle groan, Bogford raised a heavy branch and pointed behind them.

EIGHTEEN

An Unwelcome Party

It only took a moment to see what the willow was pointing at. A glowing ball of seemingly phosphorescent light was perched on a branch just behind the three friends. The glow shifted to a lower branch, which bounced slightly in response.

Now Julian began to make out the delicate form of a creature seated on the branch. Was it the Forest Fairy? He stepped closer but the ball of light flitted away. "Not this again." He turned to his friends with a sigh.

"Julian, look!" Martin pointed. The fairy had moved closer and was quite decidedly not the same one they had met earlier. This was a male fairy with a pointed, golden beard and wings considerably smaller than those of the female.

The children waited for the fairy to speak, perhaps telepathically like the other. But after a long silence it became evident that this fairy would only offer sniffs and cock-eyed stares.

Julian puffed his chest and took a step forward, just as a leader would, but something stopped him in his tracks. From every tree in the forest, phosphorescent globes were slowly emerging. Some of the orbs glowed white, others gold, cobalt blue, bright orange, rosy pink. Every color of the rainbow.

Martin took a step back. "What is happening?"

Lily couldn't help but smile as she admired the magic occurring right before her eyes.

The forest was now alight with the collective glow of the fairies. Interestingly, they moved from branch to branch, seeming to focus most of their attention on Julian, for they found him most curious of all. His funny teeth, his floppy hair, his skinny little limbs, and of course Granddad's ornate cane.

Julian ignored their pokes, prods and giggles and searched their porcelain-like faces for the one he had seen back in the valley. "Where is she?" he called out to the fairies, "Where is Florinia?"

With a tinge of jealousy in her voice, Lily answered, "Who cares? Any one of them can point us on our way."

"Florinia has gone, for now," interrupted a boyish, childlike voice telepathically from the crowd. Though all three friends heard the boyish voice clearly in their minds, none knew which fairy had transmitted it.

Julian stammered, "Um...who said that?"

No answer. Only silence – until slowly, the group of glowing fairies parted to reveal a youngling hidden protectively among them.

His glow was pure and more brilliant than all of the others' combined. He approached the children with a calm authority while the other fairies flanked him on both sides as bodyguards to a beloved boy king.

Though his childlike voice telepathically messaged each of them, his deep blue eyes focused only on Julian. "I am Eleazar. My tribe wishes to welcome you to our forest with a ceremonial celebration."

Julian was perplexed. *Why does the youngling speak on behalf of them all?* "Thank you, Eleazar. But we must turn down your offer. We are in a great hurry and haven't the time for celebrations."

Martin gave Julian a look that said *I'll handle this.* "We have business in your land, fairy. We need to get to the Lakes of Fire."

Suddenly, the glow of all the fairies dimmed at the sound of those words. They closed ranks around the youngling protectively and became jittery, some even frantic.

Eleazar came forward again and locked eyes only with Julian. "We will give you the information you seek," he messaged.

Martin smiled triumphantly.

"But only after you indulge us our tradition," Eleazar finished.

Julian sighed. What choice did they have?

Eleazar nodded ever so slightly and immediately the fairies leapt into action.

Moments later, a large bonfire was burning at the center of the clearing. The fairies had formed a circle around it and were dancing enthusiastically, causing the smoke to billow higher and higher above the dense forest.

Then a strange, intoxicating music began. Groups of particularly wild looking fairies played small fiddles crafted from tree bark with strings of spider-spun silk. Drums of leathery leaves stretched over large hollowed acorns began to beat out a mysterious rhythm.

Weird activities in a place where a 'Dark One' threatens their existence, Julian thought.

Despite the rising music, flickering flames and wafting smoke, Julian wasn't in a festive mood. He had only one thing on his mind: he must get the antique cane to Granddad before it was too late.

"Pardon me," he called to one particular fairy that danced with the grace of a ballerina under the tall, teasing flames of the bonfire. But she ignored him, so he moved to another, "Excuse me!" he called more loudly. The fairies were, however, intent on their celebration.

Julian cast Martin an uneasy look. His friend was standing very still, almost hypnotized by the fairies' song and the smoke that enveloped him.

Through the towering licks of fire and the wisps of white smoke that spiraled into impossible shapes above it, Julian could see Lily sharing a seat in yet another tree with yet another fairy. Curious, Julian moved closer. Lily and the fairy were having a conversation.

"But why do you not fly, Harmonia?" Lily asked a particularly shy little fairy next to her.

Suddenly, Harmonia's smile fell and what little glow she had to her dimmed. It was clear that Lily's question had affected her adversely.

Julian watched as Harmonia clambered up and stood on a far-reaching limb. *It's true,* Julian thought. The fairies were light as feathers but they never flew, exactly. They glided. They skimmed. But not one really took to the air.

With all her strength, the tiny fairy pushed another branch out of the way so Lily could see something.

Lily leaned forward and gasped. She looked at the fairy in horror. "The Dark One?" Lily asked incredulously.

Harmonia nodded.

To his complete surprise, Julian was suddenly tuned into their conversation - as if a switch had flipped in his mind. He could hear Harmonia's every thought directed to Lily.

After we failed him in his search for the Window in the Sky, the Dark One forbade all the forest fairies to ever fly again.

Julian chewed on the phrase, The Window in the Sky. *What could that be?* Then it clicked. *She must be talking about the portal that he entered through when he was first banished to this world. The other end of the rift!*

Lily held Harmonia's silken hand and petted it gently to comfort her.

Harmonia continued to message Lily, and Julian continued to listen in. *He took control of the island shortly after arriving, when he realized we had no leader. We had never needed one before. He brought the continual darkness with him, so it was natural that the nocturnal creatures appreciated him. He brought them all together to create his Dark Army.*

Lily became more frightened as the tale went on. Julian could see in her face that she was wishing she were back home, even if it meant being under the thumb of overprotective parents.

Harmonia continued, *When he discovered we fairies could fly, he enslaved the tribes and forced us to search every speck of sky for the Window. We wanted to find it. We wanted him to leave. But we failed and, as our punishment, he stole the Feather of Fancy from us all.* Harmonia raised one of her beautiful wings to reveal a scar where one feather had been plucked. *It is what gives flight to a fairy*, she lamented.

Julian knew exactly what must have been racing through Lily's mind right then. It had to be the same thought he was having...*The Black Taxi!*

He remembered clearly what was under its hood back at the crash site. The bundle of silken feathers as fine as he'd ever seen coated with a sparkling dust. *That's how Gabriel made his horrible craft fly!*

Harmonia was suddenly distracted. Eleazar had joined the others around the fire. Hand-in-hand, they swayed back and forth in front of the roaring flames.

The tribes chanted in unison as their energy transferred more and more heat and flame to the fire. The smoke became whiter and thicker, twisting, whirling and snaking up higher and higher into the sky.

Julian watched it intently. It was an awfully strange ceremony, he thought. *Why would a hidden tribe create such a smoky disturbance in their own forest?* Julian turned toward Martin—

But he was gone.

NINETEEN

The Oracle

She couldn't quite figure out what it was, but the curious forest fairy, Florinia, just knew that there was something different about this stranger. She had to find out.

Lost in thought, Florinia made her way to the home of the Oracle, her flowing white tunic gliding atop crystallized black desert sands that reflected the purple moonlight like infinite, little mirrors.

In the distance behind her, Florinia could faintly make out the wildly beating drums of the celebration. *What if I am right?* she panicked, *What if the stranger is the Savior*?

Florinia's heart sunk, as the drums grew louder and more insistent. She knew exactly what her tribe had in store for these strangers. All strangers had to be held for the Dark One.

She had no time to lose. She had to talk to the Oracle and make SURE that this particular stranger was, indeed, just an ordinary trespasser.

Suddenly, Florinia's thoughts were interrupted by the sound of grunting and the smell of hot, stale breath: Children of the Night. Javelinas!

Two wild boars, fangs ready with a maddened desire to pierce her tender fairy flesh, were close behind Florinia, determined to kill a fairy at long last. Partly, no doubt, because it would please their master, and partly to taste what all the fuss was about. After all, fairies were rumored to have the sweetest flesh.

The Javelinas were three times larger than any boar should ever be. With hooked, yellow fangs and hindquarters as stout as a bull's, the dreadful creatures were the Dark One's favorite beast of prey.

You only make me faster, dears, Florinia thought. She powered her wings to flutter ever quicker. She had little time before the Dark One would recognize the drum beat and send scouts to inspect the strangers.

Up ahead, shimmering in the moonlight, her destination was within sight. The green edge of an endlessly wide pond was bedecked with glittering ripples. Only these ripples didn't...ripple. They were frozen in time, glassy and smooth.

Florinia had reached the Ponderous Pond, and as much as its ambivalent nature made her uneasy, she knew she had to cross it yet again to reach the Oracle.

Florinia approached the edge of the pond. It was filled with thousands of identical pale lily pads as still as the water itself.

Faintly, in the moonlight, she could see the tiny, delicate clock faces on each lily pad. All were different but had one thing in common – they were all stopped at 12:00. Permanent midnight.

Florinia knew that to cross the Ponderous Pond she had to recall which lily pads were, in fact, disguised stones able to support the weight of any visitor who knew precisely where to step, and which were as thin as paper. But how was she to remember the riddle when every second mattered? She took a deep breath and recited its secret code inside her mind.

Right you are.

Florinia's delicate right foot, encased in a ballerina-like slipper made of rose petals, leapt quite specifically to the next lily pad. It held her weight. Florinia grinned.

When you have *left*.

With her left foot now, the next lily supported her easily.

In search of *right.*

This time, Florinia skipped two pads and landed on a third with a flourish, to the right.

To put to test.

“Oh no!” She had waited too long to move. Florinia’s tiny foot slipped and reacted with the water in a most peculiar way. She seemed not to be sinking into it – but melting into it.

To put to test!

Carefully, Lily’s ‘melting’ leg slid back to the surface of the last lily pad. She resumed reciting the remainder of the password while hopping accordingly.

If *right* is *right.*
And *left* be deft.
To *right* yourself.

She looked to her left for the final leap…

Is all that's *left.*

Each lily pad she had set upon had become the steppingstone to the next, bringing her closer to the other side of the pond where finally her feet touched solid land, and a most peculiar land it was, hard and dry, like the crackled brown skin of a crocodile.

Florinia stopped to catch her breath. She turned around to watch her overzealous pursuers, who evidently did not know the riddle of the Ponderous Pond, and struggled to mimic their prey's clever choices.

One by one, each of the Javelinas found failure by stepping onto an incorrect lily pad thereby succumbing to the volatile nature of the pond.

Despite their frantic paddling, the glassy green water around them refused to splash, wave or even ripple. Not even a single bubble rose to the surface when the last of the clumsy beasts drowned.

Florinia sighed deeply. She took no pleasure in the loss of a fellow Delphisolan, enemy or not.

Her heart beginning to beat faster with worry about the fate of the stranger, Florinia set out again, as fast as she could.

It wasn't long before she reached a chasm of indeterminable depth. And directly over that chasm hovered...the fog.

No one on the island quite understood the fog: it seemed to punish the Delphisolans at times, then at other times it was quite benevolent. Often, Florinia had heard the Gossiping Grass whisper that it was into the fog that all the goodness of the island had disappeared, long ago.

One thing Florinia did know, however, was that the fog acted as a sort of Praetorian Guard for the Oracle. And on this day it heaved rhythmically with a foreboding that Florinia had not felt in some time.

Florinia sent a telepathic thought across the chasm to the formidable guardian. *I seek the wisdom of the Oracle*, she desperately messaged.

The fog rolled more ominously, this time closing with a thunderclap. Its message was clear.

Florinia was flustered. Of all days for it to deny her access, this would not be one of them. *Please, I beg you. It is a matter of great importance to all Delphisolans.*

The fog maintained itself.

She continued, *Including Pythia. Please. This is an emergency.*

After a long pause, the fog rolled again, only this time it did not thicken; instead it dissipated entirely, revealing the scene previously hidden behind it.

A tall granite pedestal sat atop an endless pillar rising from the bottomless chasm. Seated on the pedestal, as large and wide as the pedestal's flat surface, was a lethargic, lazy-eyed red frog.

Florinia paid her respects to the sluggish, slimy amphibian with a deep bow.

It slowly lifted its heavy eyelids to half-heartedly acknowledge its visitor, but remained silent.

Florinia never understood whether the frog was stranded on the granite pedestal, essentially trapping it between both sides of the island in the very chasm that split it in two, or if it were simply unmotivated to leap far enough to land on either side.

Nonetheless, it appeared to just bathe in the vapors that rose up from the abyss and into its lungs like some mind-altering opiate.

Florinia messaged the frog. *Pythia, oh great seer of things, I come once again for your gift. I haven't much time.*

Florinia's impatience rose as the frog breathed out a long, protracted sigh and finally spoke for the first time. "Ohhh, Floriniaaaaaa.

You are a most neeeeedy little bird." Pythia's voice lingered in the air and joined the fog wafting slowly around her. It seemed to echo down into the chasm and up again.

Yes. I am sorry. But a stranger came today and—

Pythia looked up to the dark sky. "Do you know, faaaairy..." the great frog said, then inhaled for another melody, "...That I have not daaaared to leap since the Dark One arriiiived in our world and craaaaacked the land around me?"

Florinia <u>*did*</u> know this. In fact, she had heard it many times before. Something about the toxins rising from the chasm made Pythia ramble. They also somehow made her a prophet. But there was no time for this today. Florinia had to get answers. *Pythia, please...*

Pythia's bulging bloodshot eyes were slowly tracking a trio of confused fireflies that spiraled hopelessly through the toxic vapors before her. She dropped open her mouth and, with a lazy lick of her long, sticky tongue, she snatched them from the air. It was the most physical exertion Florinia had ever seen Pythia have.

Pythia chewed on the fireflies as slowly as a cow chews its cud. Their flickering light fluttered in her mouth, dimming with each crunch until extinguished altogether. Pythia grimaced. "I dooo detest the taste of those thiiiiings." She took another breath for another thought. "If not for their allegiance to the Dark One, I might not eat a siiiingle one."

Florinia wrung her hands with increasing anxiety. There wasn't time to waste.

Pythia continued her melodic exhales, "No fairy, I have nevvvver leapt...

"...And will not evvvver leap.

"...From thiiiiiis place.

"...Until Heeeeeee has leapt.

"...From ours."

There was a long pause. Long enough for Florinia to try a new tactic and message a whole thought without being interrupted. *I have news, great seer, of a stranger on our island. A new kind.*

Pythia froze in mid-yawn, caught by surprise.

Triumphantly, Florinia realized she had the Oracle's full attention. *At first, I thought it was a lost Smidgeon, perhaps, like in the old stories. But when I looked more closely, I could smell something strange. I began to think that the small, brown-haired one was the 'man' you so often told of in your prophecies.*

"The man, yes." Pythia was listening closely now.

Excited, Florinia went on. *You know, the Savior destined to come from another island to rescue us all? But then I learned that the stranger is not a man at all. He is a creature called 'boy'.*

Pythia pondered Florinia's message and rolled it over slowly in her foggy mind. "Step back, fairy," she commanded at length.

Florinia moved back farther from the chasm just as a large gust of vapors burst again into the air and wafted before Pythia. Florinia held her breath as Pythia leaned into the vapors and inhaled their toxins deeply.

Her bulbous eyes rolled back into her head until only bloodshot whiteness was left. As the toxins took effect, her plump body twitched uncontrollably in full seizure, then relaxed again. "A boy is not destined to be so forever, dove. It is said that a boy can actually become...a maaaaan."

Florinia was astounded. She lost her footing and fell to one knee. *A creature who can change?* It took her breath away. The possibility reminded her of so many tales she'd heard from the elder fairies of forgotten times when caterpillars and pollywogs could change into butterflies and toads.

"But if this chaaaaange were to happen..." Pythia continued to purge the prophecy from her writhing body, "...To this particular boy..."

She inhaled another gulp of toxins.

"If he is to become not just any man, but our Saaaavior..."

Florinia couldn't take it anymore. *Yes? Yes?*

Pythia exhaled the rest of her prophecy, "Then the chaaange shall take plaaace...when the moon's light turns black."

Florinia pondered those words. *An eclipse?*

The thought was still forming in her mind when she noticed an eclipse had already begun. The first of the three purple crescent moons above was nearly black!

Oh no! I need to get back to the forest!

TWENTY

A Total Eclipse

In the clearing of the Enchanted Forest, the twirling white smoke of Eleazar's bonfire was dissipating. The drum beats slowed, then held steady.

Julian twirled around searchingly. Where had Martin gone?

Lily was still sitting in the tree with the innocent Harmonia when, suddenly, a shrill piercing sound shook the forest.

Instantly, the fairies all dimmed and fled back into the shadows. Something was coming. And it was overhead.

"Help!"

Julian looked up to see one of the scariest, weirdest things he'd ever seen. Martin was dangling from the claws of a pterodactyl-sized bat flying over him!

"Let me go!" Martin shouted, terrified.

Julian looked around for something – anything - to throw at the bat. He found a rock nearby and hurled it as hard as he could. With a shriek, the bat let go of Martin and flew away to nurse the lump in its head, caused by the rock.

Moments later after Martin recovered from his fall, another shriek sounded. With quick thinking, Julian tackled Martin and Lily just in time to avoid the swooping of another mammoth bat that had whizzed into the clearing like a warplane. It had plunged straight down the opening in the tree cover spiraling just as swiftly as the smoke had earlier twirled upward. Their horrid shrieks echoed terror throughout the forest.

"Hide!" Julian shouted to Lily and Martin as the bats orchestrated another attack.

Lily and Martin were able to scatter into the brush, like so many fairies had, and Julian was just about to do the same when he noticed the shy fairy, Harmonia, exposed to the danger from an opening in the branches. She sat naively calm on the limb, watching the bats curiously as if she were being entertained.

The bats noticed her, too. Like perfectly piloted jets in an air show, they circled back with wondrous symmetry and zeroed in on their newfound, little target.

As the swooping carnivores were headed straight for the tiny Harmonia, Julian did the only thing he could think of, "Here goes nothing." Julian pointed Granddad's time-bending cane at the bats and shouted, "Freeze!"

And they did!

Martin came out of the shrubs to marvel at the beasts frozen just above them in midair. He waved his arms around them like a magician after a trick to prove there were no wires.

Just like poor Linus, under the blanket down in the Keepers' Chamber, the bats were now suspended in time, catatonic - as if their own personal clocks had simply stopped ticking.

Eleazar's stomach sank, his breathing stopped momentarily. Nearby, another fairy sensed their leader's shock and stayed glued to the youngling, waiting for his command.

All was quiet until Lily suddenly appeared with a slap across Julian's wrist, dropping Freemont's cane to the ground.

"What was that for?" Julian cried out.

"Don't you ever scare us like that again, Rigby. What were you thinking, taking such a foolish risk?" she asked, trembling.

"I was thinking that someone had to stop them," Julian sincerely responded.

"Well then, Jules, mission accomplished," Martin smirked.

Martin gently lifted Granddad's cane and inspected it. He held it high like the mighty sword Excalibur, and then waved it around, forcing the others to duck. "How did you do it, Jules? I want to try," he begged.

"Careful with that, Martin," Julian warned. "I'm not even sure myself how it works."

Lily kept on with worry, "Julian, you nearly gave me a heart attack." She hugged him as tight as she could. For Julian there was no better feeling in this world or any other.

Meanwhile, Martin reenacted the scene like a swashbuckling pirate. He whirled the cane around and pointed at the familiar black crow that was once again circling overhead. "Freeze!" he commanded, but the crow kept circling.

Frustrated, Martin pointed the cane at the frozen bat scouts and shouted again, "Freeze! I command you to freeze!"

They remained just as they were.

"You see that, Jules? I think I just made them freeze even more than they were already freezing. Do they appear somehow freezier to you?"

Lily rolled her eyes.

Martin scrambled to gather vines from the nearby trees so he could tie up the frozen beasts. They would be his prisoners of war.

Slowly, several of the forest fairies began to come out of hiding – awestruck by what they had witnessed.

First there were five. Then ten. Twenty. And even more. They grew in numbers much larger than were originally at the bonfire celebration. There must have been two hundred in all in their tribe.

As Martin finished wrapping the vines around the creatures stalled in mid-air, Lily turned Julian around to see that the fairies were no longer staring at the creatures he had frozen.

They were staring at him.

They sniffed his aura. They examined him carefully. They pointed at him as if he were some sculpture in a museum or some riddle to be solved, and he could feel that they were secretly messaging one another.

"I know what you're thinking," he spoke aloud. "I know this looks strange."

"Um... Julian?" Martin called from behind.

Julian continued addressing the crowd of fairies, "Trust me, I don't quite understand it, myself."

"Julian?" Martin called with more urgency.

Julian and Lily turned to see what Martin was so nervously warning them about. The time spell was loosening its hold on the bats and they were starting to thaw from their frozen state.

The fairies buzzed around nervously, urging Julian to do something, but there wasn't enough time.

Before Martin could finish tying the final knot, the bats had wiggled partially free of their bondage.

Eeeeeeeek!

That familiar horrid shriek filled the air as the larger of the two bats shook off one of the vines, throwing Martin back against the thick trunk of a tree. It spat in all directions as it wrestled with the remaining vines. A splash of saliva landed on a large brown leaf near Julian and burned through it like acid. "That's not good."

The larger bat flew at Martin in a rage.

Martin lifted Freemont's cane in the air and then he pointed it with great conviction at the beast shouting, "Freeze!"

But the cane's magic did not work this time, and the savage beast surged viciously toward its kill.

Julian and Lily stood helpless as it unlocked its jaws and revealed fearsome fangs ready to seize their friend.

Within a hair of reaching Martin, it was yanked back by the tangle of one of the vines and forced into a spin that jerked it straight into the trunk of the forest's largest willow, splitting its skull and landing it flat on its back at the feet of a breathless Martin.

The willow came alive just as Bogford and Mergda had done earlier and boomed triumphantly, “Take that, Children of the Night!”

Martin sighed with relief. His life had been spared, at least for now.

The beast twitched at his feet many times before finally dying.

This prompted a guttural moan from its partner who watched it all while still thawing and trying to wiggle free of its own vines. The sorrowful moans turned quickly into angry shrieks as it attempted to break free and flap its vast wings of vengeance.

Martin threw the cane to Julian and screamed, “Quick, cast another spell!”

Julian stood before the remaining beast as it wiggled free and righted itself. He raised the cane, pointed it at the bat and...drew a blank!

Nothing came out. No words. No thoughts. Nothing!

The beast flapped its awful wings and lunged for the boy who kept pointing the cane, speechless.

Julian closed his eyes and thought of Granddad.

Suddenly, he was jolted by a force that nearly shattered his bony arms. Then came an absolutely deafening shriek that exploded from the beast and cracked the sky like lightning. It was so loud that it traveled the entire island, pricking the ears of every creature.

Even Pythia had awakened from her toxic slumber.

And Gabriel, who was walking with his much fatigued prisoner under the darkest of night skies, their path lighted by the escort of a thousand obedient fireflies, stopped to ponder the sound.

Finally, Julian opened his eyes and saw that Granddad's cane had speared the beast right through its heart.

The bat sat slumped before him like a slain dragon, every heave of its impaled chest weaker than the last one.

Martin, Lily and Julian turned to see the hundreds of fairies circling Julian and bowing to him. Their collective glow lit his confused, boyish face.

Then Eleazar calmly approached. *You must accept our sincerest apology, Julian. Had we known it was you, we never would have summoned the scouts.*

"Summoned the scouts? What are you talking about?"

Eleazar messaged back, *It is the law of our land to notify the Dark One of any strangers, especially those who take your form. But had we known then what we know now, Julian...*

"Notify the Dark One? Wait a minute! Is that what your little welcome party was? The smoke you sent up through the trees? Was that a signal? You called those bats to come get me?"

Fairies pawed at Julian's face, tugged at his clothes. Their happy glow was dizzying.

Eleazar scrambled to clarify, *Julian, you don't understand. What you've just done with your magic cane—*

"The cane is not even mine!" Julian shouted, burning with anger. He spun around, desperate to find his friends. Where *was* the cane, anyway?

Eleazar sent another message. *Worry not. The Gossiping Grass carries word that the Oracle has foretold of your transformation during an eclipse. Soon, all the prophecies will come true. Soon...*

Julian's eyes followed Eleazar's pointed finger up toward the sky and saw, not just that all of the moons were nearly eclipsed, but more importantly, that the silhouette of one of the defeated bats was flying away, and still stuck in its chest, was Granddad's time-altering cane.

TWENTY-ONE

Finders, Keepers

In the same dark cell that once held Julian for an excruciating three hours, Sir Alfred waited patiently.

He leaned against the solid steel door using what little light spilled in through a rectangular-shaped slot to read the pages of his Keepers' Bible.

But not everyone in Westminster's Station #5 was as calm, cool and collected as Sir Alfred. In fact, even its officers had probably never been more preoccupied, stressed or downright stupefied as they were on this day.

Through the slot, Sir Alfred watched an officer escort a thoroughly confused Zulu warrior in full battle regalia to a cell. *First the wombat and the chameleon. Now this?*

The rift, it seemed, was leaking.

Phones rang. Papers were shuffled. Shoes squeaked frantically on the terrazzo floors.

Sir Alfred's index finger, still stained from fingerprint ink, gently turned another page of his Keepers' Bible.

He stopped reading for a moment to consider Julian. He hoped that the boy was having more luck in the other dimension than he and Bishop were having in this one. In the time that Julian had been gone, Sir Alfred and Bishop were no closer to discovering the location of the Sacred Object, and had now found themselves behind bars for, as Detective Riley put it, 'Harboring a dangerous whatch-a-mathingy.'

Perhaps it was too late, Sir Alfred thought, and closed his eyes.

Suddenly, the shadows grew darker as an officer approached Sir Alfred's cell, blocking out the only bit of light he had. He opened his eyes, closed his book and peered through the opening but could only see the man's midsection.

The officer's arms were full of random objects sealed in translucent bags, all labeled alphabetically.

Among them, Sir Alfred recognized many of the objects from the clock shop. Broken pieces of white walnut that once formed Freemont's precious Little Big Ben huddled like frightened children in one bag. Freemont's door chimes jingled like fire alarms in another, and the switch to the silent alarm laid quiet in a third bag, labeled only as ‘C’.

To Sir Alfred this was a most bizarre collection of ‘evidence’ these officers had chosen to gather. It illustrated how desperate they were to find any clue to give meaning to the rift they had discovered in the cellar. Sir Alfred took great comfort in these symbols of their despair.

“Jefferson!” called a woman’s raspy voice from down the hall.

The officer pivoted on his squeaky heels, losing his grip on the evidence bags that slid down his body as he struggled to hold on. His voice was pitchy and flustered, “Me?”

The raspy woman responded with a flavorful condescension clearly implying that today was not the day for stupid questions, “You see any other Jeffersons around? And no, I don’t mean the Thomas Jefferson wacko that was brought in earlier claiming to be from another time.”

Sir Alfred watched the officer’s body slump in defeat. “Can you just tell me what you want, Miriam? I’ve got to get all this over to Evidence, or Riley will have m’head.” The bags continued to slip from his grasp.

“Call on line two.”

“I’m a little busy right—”

“Your wife. She’s been watching the news.”

More interesting than the awkward dance the officer performed was what Sir Alfred saw behind him in the rectangular slot of the cell across the hall.

It was the familiar white furry face of Petey; Bishop's pestering pet ferret, and Sir Alfred knew very well what both Petey and his master were up to.

As the officer stammered with indecision and frustration, and his evidence bags slipped and slid from his grip, Petey darted out, plundered, and delivered the bags, one by one, to the slot of Bishop's cell door. The little fur ball even stole the officer's canister of pepper spray from his belt.

"Oy!" The officer reacted to the sight of a scaly woman with flowing red hair being carried down the hall by another officer.

Sir Alfred cringed. *Was that a mermaid just gone by?*

"Oy! Has she checked in?" The officer forgot about his missing evidence bags and ran down the hall after the mermaid, as fast as his awkward body would carry him.

Once the hallway was clear, Sir Alfred whispered across to the opposite cell, "Bishop? That you in there?"

"Who wants to know?"

"Have you gone mad? Stealing evidence now?"

An unintelligible grunt echoed from inside Bishop's cell. "Ah, what more could they do to us, brother? They're about to unlock the secrets to the Society and destroy all we've worked for, lived for."

"They're not going to unlock anything. They've got nothing."

"They've got the rift!" barked Bishop grumpily.

"Yes, but they don't understand what it is. Besides, they'll never be able to link it to a society they don't even know exists. It's up to us to—" Sir Alfred could see directly into Bishop's cell. Something else had the scientist's attention now. From one of the bags, Bishop pulled out the tubular sign that had once hung over the front door of the clock shop, the one that read, *'Time and tide wait for no man.'*

Petey pawed at it like a kitten with a ball of yarn until...

CLINK-CLINK!

It made a strange sound.

Sir Alfred gasped. "It's got something inside, Bishop!"

Bishop unraveled the two pieces of the tube slowly to extend the papyrus scroll that had been hidden inside. Calligraphy-inked words were scribbled from end to end.

"What is it, mate?" Sir Alfred whispered.

"Exhibit G is what the fine officers of Westminster Station #5 would call it. But to you and me, I'd say it's some sort of...chart."

"A chart?" whispered Sir Alfred. "Of the Society? An org chart?"

Bishop grimaced, "How could I have missed this before? I checked every square inch of that place, even the tank of the toilet. And these hopeless clowns..."

Sir Alfred tried to keep him focused. "What does it say, Bishop?"

"I don't know. It's in Latin."

Sir Alfred whispered back, "Have Petey run it over."

Quick as lightning, the tiny ferret delivered the parchment to Sir Alfred, who took it from him disgustedly. "Filthy creature, Bishop. Really."

Bishop murmured back, "Did you know that Mozart took much of his inspiration from a three-year relationship with a pet bird? Great men, Sir Alfred. All had great pets."

Sir Alfred had heard it all before. He ignored Bishop and carefully unrolled the scroll.

"What do you see?" Now it was Bishop's turn to wait.

Sir Alfred unraveled the scroll just a bit and struggled to read it due to the light from his cell door being overshadowed by passersby. "Well, there are lines going in many directions with just as many names alongside them. English surnames, like Beardsley and Durwood, Ravenger and Lansdon." Sir Alfred pondered them all. "Durwood sounds familiar. Ravenger, too, I suppose. They sound like the names of Keepers of centuries ago. Senior Keepers."

"How do they appear on the chart?" Bishop asked.

"In groupings. Beardsley and Durwood are together then below on a separate line are Ravenger and Landsdon. But there are hundreds more." Sir Alfred scrutinized the strange document carefully, unraveling more and more, and his heart began to beat a little more heavily. Something about this discovery felt very important indeed.

"What else?" Bishop pressed, barely able to contain his growing excitement.

"It seems to be charting the passage of power through time from one Senior Keeper to the next," whispered Sir Alfred, glancing up to make sure the coast was still clear. "The names must be grouped with their spouses," he continued, "But only one of each grouping is labeled with text. Difficult to read."

He adjusted his glasses and squinted, angling the paper for as much light as he could garner from the slotted door. “Primorus Prognatus.” He stopped, gasped slightly, and let that phrase settle in his mind.

“Translation?” Bishop became frustrated at the intellectual investigation Sir Alfred was hosting all on his own.

“First born,” Sir Alfred replied, as if in a dream. “Let me see whose name is at the very top.”

There was a long silence. Bishop craned his head to try to see Sir Alfred, but it was no use. “Sir Alfred! What is the name at the top?”

Sir Alfred struggled to find it. “Patris.”

Bishop scratched his head. “Doesn’t sound familiar.”

Awestruck, Sir Alfred put down the parchment. “Oh my. Bishop, Patris is Latin for...the Father.”

Bishop gasped. “So it is true, then? The Society *does* date back to the Father? It’s not just legend after all. Each of these Keepers protected time for centuries. Keeping it linear and whole. Keeping all dimensions separated from each other, and keeping all life moving forward.”

Sir Alfred was too lost in thought to reply for a moment. Then something hit him. “Wait.

Wait. Wait, Bishop." Sir Alfred scrambled through his blazer pockets and pulled out the folded up portrait – the one they had discovered hidden by the sands of time that poured through the bottleneck of Freemont's 24-Hour Glass.

Sir Alfred unfolded the portrait and stared at it for the hundredth time. The old bearded man, Father Time, holding the little Baby New Year. "Bishop, recite to me again the coded phrase we deciphered back at the shop, and do it slowly."

Bishop obliged, one word at a time. "What. Makes. Us. Tick. Is. Most. Sacred. Of. All."

Sir Alfred's eyes zeroed in on a surprising little detail in the portrait that he had not previously noticed: it was the direction the old man's eyes were looking ...toward the chest of the baby boy. He whispered the phrase again, "What makes us tick is most sacred of all."

That image of the baby boy, protectively covering his own chest with leaves held by his own hands – suddenly it all made sense!

"The heart!" Sir Alfred gasped. "The heart is what makes us tick. It is what is most sacred of all."

"What are you talking about, Sir Alfred?"

"And – what's this?" Sir Alfred peered at the document very carefully. Sir Alfred's brain was moving faster than his lips were able to. His calm demeanor was washed away with a stammering more reminiscent of one of Detective Riley's Keystone Cops. "At the bottom of the d-document! It says s-sangue de sangue!"

This still meant nothing to Bishop.

"Blood of my blood. Bishop, the words under each of the Senior Keeper's names are Primorus Prognatus, which means…First Born."

"You already told me that, old man," Bishop grumped.

"Blood of my blood," Sir Alfred repeated. He continued, "This is no org chart, friend. 'Tis a family tree!"

Instantly, everything clicked into place for Bishop. "What makes us tick is most SACRED of all. The Sacred Object is not an object at all. It is something in the heart of man, passed through time from the very beginning, from the Father to his firstborn child, and to every one thereafter!"

Both men were nearly paralyzed with an intuitive foreboding of what they were about to discover.

Bishop just had to know. "Sir Alfred, tell me. What is the last name written at the bottom of the scroll?"

Sir Alfred unraveled the scroll further, revealing more names. Then he saw one that struck him dumb. He laid his hand on his

Keepers' Bible and closed his old eyes. "What have we done?"

"What, old friend? What?" Bishop asked impatiently.

"The last name on the list is Julian Rigby."

TWENTY-TWO

A Friendly Chat

Julian stood uncomfortably as hundreds of pairs of fairy eyes stared at him expectantly. Julian knew he was no savior. He couldn't even keep track of a cane.

One fairy came forward and delicately touched the hem of his short pants.

"Make them stop it!" Julian grumbled to Eleazar. He had to get that cane back, and find Granddad.

They are ready to bear witness to your metamorphosis, Julian. The last moon will darken in just moments and the Oracle says that you will become a...

"A what? A lion? An eagle? A fire-breathing dragon?"

A man, Eleazar messaged.

A long pause was followed by a dismissive chuckle from Julian. *Ah, yes.* How could he have not seen that coming? It's what everyone had been telling him for years. One day he would be a man. *And then what?* he thought, *All of my problems would magically go away? Would my mum and dad come back? Would the nightmares end?* "What is so bloody great about being a man?" he barked.

Then, at that exact moment, the third crescent moon was eclipsed. And absolutely nothing happened to Julian.

The fairies let out a collective sigh of disappointment.

Julian locked eyes with Florinia, freshly returned from her visit with The Oracle. "I am no one's savior. I am only an orphan boy who is afraid of the dark."

Eleazar messaged Julian once more. *But your powers? You stopped the Dark One's scouts in mid-air. Froze them in time. How, Julian?*

"Are you all so eager for a savior that you can't see what is so clearly in front of you? It was the cane, you fools! The cane holds the magic powers of time. And now, because of you all, it is gone!" Julian turned and walked away, angry and embarrassed. He was no man. That was for sure.

Martin and Lily went after their humiliated friend, but he ran too quickly, and soon the friends lost sight of him.

Devastated by the fairies' betrayal and the loss of Granddad's magic cane, Julian now sat alone, sulking, inside Gabriel's abandoned Black Taxi, right where he and his friends had left it – crashed in the valley at the foot of the hills.

He sat there for what seemed like hours, but who knows how long it was in a land without time? Julian suddenly felt Lily and Martin staring at him from nearby. He knew that they wanted to say something, to do something, anything...to help him right now.

But the truth was, there was no helping Julian. Not anymore.

Lily tapped on the driver's side window. "Julian? Julian?"

He wouldn't even look at her.

"Leave him be," answered Martin. "What he needs right now is just a little bit of time."

Time. Time!

There it was again, that horrible word.

That stupid notion that time somehow can magically heal people. No one knew that to be poppycock more than Julian. Time had healed nothing for him. It had only exacerbated his pain.

Once again, Lily's voice came muffled through the glass. "You don't have to speak to me, but will you at least pop the hood?"

Julian's left hand calmly obliged her, while his eyes stared blankly ahead.

After the hood was unhinged, Julian could barely make out Martin's voice saying, "Oh, I see. You want ol' Winkleman to fix the flying machine, is that right, Lily? Well, I'll give it a shot but I can't make any promises."

"My hero," Lily answered sarcastically, as she pushed up her sleeves and readied herself for the task instead.

As the two of them lifted the hood and began looking around, Julian stared and stared…at his own reflection in the rearview mirror.

He stared at his face. Oh, how he hated that face – the unruly brown curls of hair, the goofy front teeth more suited to a man twice his size. He hated everything about his reflection right now. "This is all your fault," he said to his hate-able face. "Well? What have you to say for yourself?"

His face stared back at him but offered nothing.

"Speak up! Say something!"

Suddenly, a voice did answer. A shaky little voice that spoke to him in rhyme.

"Would sorry suffice?
If I said it real nice?"

It was Wilfred, the caterpillar! He was alive and well but near blind without his glasses.

Julian took one look at the tiny creature peeking out from the heater vent of the dashboard and shouted, "Ah!"

Wilfred, eyes squinted and useless, was startled by the boy's scream, so he did the same, "Ah!"

Julian was further startled by the confirmation of a talking caterpillar inside the car, so he shouted again, "Ah!"

Wilfred grew ever more frantic with each scream. "Ah! Ah! WHY ARE WE SCREAMING!?"

Alarmed, Martin popped his head out from behind the hood of the taxi. "You okay in there, Jules?"

Julian inspected the fuzzy little insect. He figured it posed no threat. He cracked the driver's window a bit to answer, "Yes. I um, just stubbed my toe."

Martin furrowed his brow, confused. "Right. Hate when that happens." He went back to the front of the car, fiddling with random parts he didn't understand. "Maybe we should check the wiper fluid," he said to Lily.

Julian could hear the frustration in Lily's tone. "Wiper fluid, Third? Really?" She shouted back to Julian, "Go ahead. Give it a turn."

Julian was too mesmerized by his tiny talking visitor to understand her. "Huh?"

"The key. Give it a turn."

Julian twisted the key in the ignition.

RE-RE-RE-RE-RE-RE-RE

No luck. "Who are you, little caterpillar?" Julian inquired.

Wilfred tried to point his face in the direction of Julian's voice, but without his glasses he could never quite find the source.

"Friends of mine, they call me Will.
I live inside the grinding mill.
Or did, at least, until this day.
But now, I fear, I am astray."

Julian found himself slightly amused by Wilfred. His penchant for rhyme reminded Julian of Granddad, but that sweet memory only made Julian feel angrier and more hopeless about the mess he'd gotten himself into. "Well, Will. I am Julian. Julian Rigby."

The furry little insect gasped, and no more did he indulge in rhyme. "Forgive me, Mr. Julian, but mine eyes are fickle. What manner of creature are you?"

"I am a boy," Julian answered definitively, "And do not dispute it or I shall—"

"Oh, dear."

"What?"

"Oh, dear. Oh, my. Oh, gosh. Oh, no!" The little caterpillar was definitely troubled. He paced back and forth along the dashboard, bumping into knobs and switches.

Julian could see the worry in his fuzzy little brow. *But why is Will so worried?*

"Give it another try, Jules!" shouted Lily from behind the hood.

RE-RE-RE-RE-RE-RE-RE-RE

Nothing. A few random drops of rain spat on Martin's platinum hair. "Perfect, just what we need right now," complained Martin.

Julian noticed the windshield of the taxi becoming streaked with raindrops. They were an electric yellow and as they traveled the glass they left wiggly trails that defied gravity. "Why have you quieted yourself?" Julian questioned his new companion.

Wilfred lifted one of his many little limbs to his mouth, "Shh. I hear voices."

He did. But they were only Martin and Lily, arguing under the hood.

"Do you know what you're doing there?" Martin nagged. "This isn't something girls typically understand. Why don't you step aside and let me—"

"Will you shut up, already?" snapped Lily.

"No, I won't."

"But I insist."

"Insist all you want but I'm tired of listening to you."

Julian explained to the confused and nearly blind caterpillar, "It's just my stupid friends being stupid."

But Wilfred kept his head held high and his body leaned toward the sound. "Listen more closely and you might hear more, Mr. Julian."

As the rain fell harder, Julian listened again.

"You think I don't know this is my fault?" Martin shouted. "Well, guess what? I do!"

"What are you talking about?" Lily scoffed.

Martin admitted, "I wanted so badly to prove that I was more than just another Winkleman legacy. I pressured you both to come so that I could finally have my own story to tell."

Julian could hear the shame in his friend's voice. It saddened him even more.

Then Lily fired back. "That's ridiculous. If this is anyone's fault, it's mine. I wanted to get out of the house. I wanted to meet interesting people. I wanted to be free of my parents' tight control."

Wilfred shook his tiny head. "I may be blind, Mr. Julian, but even I can see that you are all a bit confused. You say it's your fault, they say it's theirs."

"Well *I'm* not confused, Will. They're wrong. It is my fault. And only my fault. The magic cane is gone because of me. Granddad is gone because of me." Julian's voice cracked as he pushed out the last words, "My mum and dad are gone – because of me!"

Wilfred did not need to see Julian to know he was crying, and as a tear trickled down the boy's face, so did the yellow rain trickle down the windshield, harder now than before. Somehow, the droplets chased down every bit of dirt and grime, washing away the past.

Breaking the near silence of the moment was Lily's voice coming from behind the hood, "Martin, I need your help," Lily admitted softly.

"You do?"

"Put your finger here. And hold this metal part here."

"Like this?"

"Yes. Now, I need your belt."

"What?"

"I promise, it's not a trick. May I take it?"

"Go ahead. I trust you."

Wilfred stood up on his back sets of legs to hear better what was happening. He smiled sweetly. "It seems they have figured out that you are much stronger together than alone, Mr. Julian."

"With all due respect, Will, you are but a myopic caterpillar from another world. You know nothing about me or what makes me better off."

"I know more about you, and your parents, than you think, Mr. Julian."

Julian's mouth dropped open. *What was he talking about?*

"Who are you? What do you know about my parents?" Julian demanded. "Is this some sort of sick joke? All you creatures on this island are twisted. Do you know that? You're twisted!"

Wilfred interjected calmly, "I speak only truth, Mr. Julian. I know the secrets of your Granddad. I know that your parents loved you deeply. And I know, for a fact, that they are gone not because of you, dear boy. They are gone because of..." Then, for the first time, Wilfred looked in the direction he intended, straight at the orange embers that glowed across the island, the same glowing embers that Harmonia had pointed them to from her tree in the Enchanted Forest, "Him."

The rain pounded the windshield now. Lily shouted louder than ever from under the hood, "Julian! Give it one more try!"

Julian stared at Wilfred. He was confused but for some reason, he believed the caterpillar. He believed that he did somehow understand the boy. That he did know the truth.

Lily repeated herself, "Julian! Give it a go! You must try one more time. Just try!"

Wilfred nodded at Julian. They were right. He had to try. He extended his right arm and twisted the key again.

RE-RE-RE-RE-RE-RE-VROOOOOM!

It started! The Black Taxi was fixed! The slightest grin curled Julian's lip; Lily and Martin jumped and danced victoriously; and suddenly, the pouring rain stopped.

They looked at the Black Taxi. It was shining clean for the very first time.

Julian popped open the driver's door and looked at Martin confidently. "Well, what are you waiting for, Winkleman? This thing's not going to fly itself."

Martin and Lily excitedly jumped into the taxi, and then Martin readied himself at the controls.

The windshield wipers cleared a line of sight onto Gabriel's lair in the distance. Julian once again felt anger growing inside him.

He knew Wilfred had told the truth. It was Gabriel who was responsible for his parents' death, and now it was time Julian had his vengeance. "Guys, say hello to Will."

Wilfred popped back out from the heating vent.

"Allow me to greet you.
'Tis a pleasure to meet you."

"What the heck? Where'd that come from?" laughed Lily with surprise.

"Yeah, who is he?" asked Martin.

"He came from the grinding mill, and he..." Julian lifted the little caterpillar and carefully set him inside his shirt pocket, "...Is my pet. All great men have one."

Martin and Lily smiled and welcomed Julian's new sidekick.

"Nice to meet you, little Will. I am Lady Lily."

"And I'm Sir Martin, of the Winkleman Clan," laughed Martin.

Julian buckled his seat belt and took a breath. "Oh, by the way, what was wrong with the engine?"

Lily answered, "You're not going to believe it."

"Try me."

"It was the timing belt!"

VROOOM!

Just like the mechanisms on Julian's roller shoes, the wheels of the Black Taxi slid up to the sides and disappeared as the flying craft rose up from the ground and soared away...
...Followed by a single, black crow.

TWENTY-THREE

A Royal Disaster

Detective Riley planted himself firmly outside the front door of the AM/PM Emporium.

Across from Detective Riley, an egg-shaped blowhard in a three-piece suit and an ill-fitting toupee was rambling on about politics when, suddenly, he was drowned out by the roar of a dozen mega-sized diesel engines in an approaching caravan of military vehicles.

The crushing weight of their steel frames on the small, pedestrian-only cobblestone street was enough to rattle the ground beneath Detective Riley and his chatterbox friend. Eleven camouflaged combat trucks and one green Land Rover with tinted windows pulled to a stop.

Two soldiers in fatigues exited the Land Rover in perfect symmetry and step. While one stood guard, the other opened the back passenger door.

A spit-shined boot, with perfectly tied laces, attached to a very fit and very neat man in his fifties, stepped out. The man's military uniform was immaculate, from the bright colors of his stripes to the glint of every badge and pin. His salt-and-pepper hair was equally subordinate, without so much as a single strand daring to break form, and the smooth skin on his chiseled face looked as if it had just been shaved clean on the way over.

The man marched up to Riley and his egg-shaped companion with a soldier flanking him at each side. "You Detective Riley?" he asked, barely moving his rigid upper lip.

"I am," Riley answered.

The uniformed man kept his eyes locked on the detective. "Who is the clown in the monkey suit and why is he blocking my path to the door?"

The bloated man gasped, "Why, I never!"

"And he never will." The uniformed man continued to look only at the detective.

The bloated man straightened himself up and lifted his head high. "I beg your pardon sir, but I just happen to be the Right Honourable Lord Mayor of London who has sworn allegiance to the Sovereign in the presence of our notable judges of the High Court to…"

The uniformed man slowly cocked his neck to one side until it cracked loudly. His eyes never left Detective Riley as he spoke next.

"Someone pull the batteries from this puppet. If I hear it squeak again, it will be tossed into the Thames."

With a slight nod, Detective Riley motioned for the Lord Mayor to give the uniformed man some space.

"Listen up, Detective. I'm only going to say this once so take notes, record it on your cell phone or even tattoo it on your bum if you must. I don't care."

"I'm sure I'll remember it." Detective Riley leaned forward.

"Good. I am Colonel Chadwick Burroughs of the Royal British Brigade. I've been appointed by the Prime Minister, that's the people's Prime Minister, your Prime Minister, to handle all security matters to ensure the absolute safety of our nation at any and all cost."

Detective Riley knew what was coming next and wished that the colonel would skip the formality and just say it. Instead, he waited patiently as the colonel continued to drop names and titles.

"This morning I sat in a conference with the Prime Minister, Secretary of Defense and Head of Intelligence. We reviewed the video your men sent of the..." He sniffed the air, searching for the right word. "...Unidentified Floating Object. Subsequently, I was instructed to travel here immediately and take over command of this location in the interest of protecting the security of the people from...well, said floating object."

Detective Riley was surprised by how little the military seemed to know of what 'it' was.

"In short, Detective, I'm King Kong and this is my skyscraper now."

The sputtering Lord Mayor interjected, "You were sent to protect the people? But how do you know they are even in danger?"

Colonel Burroughs took an intentionally loud deep breath and ignored the Lord Mayor completely. "What you have discovered, Detective Riley, is not of this world. Think on that for a bit."

Detective Riley acknowledged his point with a subtle glance.

"But don't think on it here." The man saluted the Detective swiftly, "You are dismissed."

Detective Riley returned the Colonel's salute and smiled to himself, proud to have been part of such a big discovery. *This just might be the career move I've been waiting for*, he thought, *Something to define my life's work.* Riley's reverie was broken by a shout.

"Collister!"

One of the military officers flanking the Colonel obediently shuffled forward. "Sir!"

"Send in the EOD unit immediately. Time to sweep up this mess."

The chastened Lord Mayor skulked nearby, his toupee sliding into an odd angle. "May I ask, Colonel...what is E.O.D.?"

Detective Riley guided the Lord Mayor out of the way as soldiers jumped back into action. "It's the, um..." Riley started to explain, and then he noticed something quite remarkable from the corner of his eye.

It was an Ammunition Tech Officer (ATO) bouncing toward them from the last truck, fully suited with so much padding and armor that he looked like a big, puffy astronaut walking on the moon.

The rest of the men cheered him on and slapped his back as he walked down the aisle of their adulation.

Detective Riley finished his reply, "Explosive Ordnance Disposal."

"Explosive Ordnance Disposal? What are they here for?"

The detective couldn't take his eyes off the man in the padded suit. "It looks as though they intend to detonate...*it*."

"I can see how you attained your position, Detective. You're a keen little cucumber, aren't you?" Colonel Burroughs injected sarcastically.

The Lord Mayor continued with his curious questions, "Before studying it? You're going to detonate it before even studying it?"

Colonel Burroughs pointedly ignored the Mayor and instead bore his steely eyes into Detective Riley. "We studied your video and made an executive decision. Now clear your men out or I will have them all detained for interrupting a military operation. I don't want to see - or even hear - a single living, breathing organism within 100 meters of this establishment. Are we clear?"

Detective Riley couldn't put his finger on it, but suddenly he wasn't feeling quite so good about Burroughs and whatever he was up to. "Clear."

"Then move!" Burroughs turned to the Lord Mayor, acknowledging him for the first time. "Except you, puppet. You stay."

"Me? Why?"

The Colonel shouted over his shoulder. "COLLISTER!"

The same officer flanking him at his side shuffled forward once again. "Sir!"

"What did I say would happen if I heard one more squeak from this puppet?"

Officer Collister shouted back with just as much gusto. "He would be tossed into the Thames, sir!"

"Correct. So why is he standing so close to me that I can smell the foul stench of his fear?"

Officer Collister wasn't sure how to respond. "Uh...I will escort him out of your way—"

The Colonel interrupted loudly, "You will toss him into the river!"

Officer Collister glanced over at the officer flanking the Colonel's other side, wondering what to do.

"Now!" shouted the Colonel.

Apologetically, the two officers lifted the Lord Mayor by his arms and legs and struggled to carry the awkwardly overweight fellow across the cobblestone street toward the bridge as he pled for them to reconsider.

Colonel Burroughs watched with a slight smirk as the Lord Mayor was thrown off the bridge for a mid-afternoon dip in the Thames. "Excellent. Now, Detective Riley, we've got to—"

But when Burroughs looked back, Detective Riley was gone.

TWENTY-FOUR

A Keeper's Oath

Back in jail, more and more strange characters were being brought in. One particularly muscular man even called himself by the name of Hercules, but Sir Alfred paid him no mind. No, he had a question for his partner in crime. "Bishop!"

"What?"

"What happens if another one of them goes inside?"

Bishop's usual fluttering about suddenly ceased upon the gravity of the question. "Inside what, the rift? Well, I suppose it depends on their size and the current state of the rift. Someone the size of a child, like Julian, well, they'd have great odds to survive the travel."

"Yes, but let us assume that the British authorities won't be sending children inside. What then?"

Bishop slid down the inside of his cell door, forced to imagine the scientific probability of that scenario. It quieted him. "Well, as I tried to explain before...depending on if the rift is expanding or contracting...that could be problematic." He curled his nose at the thought, pondering a gruesome demise or, at the very least, torture. "If improperly positioned during travel, it is quite possible they could be spaghettified."

"Explain to me what that means again," Sir Alfred asked gently, bracing himself for the answer.

"It's all about position. For example, if they travel through on their backs like on a water slide, with their feet ahead of them and arms over their heads – then it is likely they will experience an extreme pulling sensation at their extremities. They will feel like they are on a medieval stretching device literally being torn apart."

Sir Alfred buried his head in his hands. "And otherwise?"

"If they are curled up in a more fetal position, it is conceivable that any limb or part of the body that doesn't fit in the core of the tunnel and protrudes too far out near the edges, where the pulling force is strongest, would be...warped."

"Warped?"

"Look, it's all theoretical, Sir Alfred. There exists no such data to say for certain. Real live rifts aren't exactly well documented in the scientific community. But suffice it to say that serious complications could occur."

Sir Alfred had heard enough bad news for one day. He simply couldn't endure any more blood on his hands. "This is most regrettable, old friend," he sighed deeply. "A Keeper's Oath is made to all creatures in all realms of the Father. It is done. We must tell them."

Like a splash of cold water to the face, Bishop was startled by Sir Alfred's words. "What? Are you hearing yourself? What could we possibly tell them? That what they are looking at is actually the world's only traversable wormhole? Think about that, Sir Alfred. Their narrow little minds would explode!"

Suddenly, a voice broke through their frantic whispers. "Better our minds than the very thing itself."

The two old men remained quiet as a familiar fire hydrant-shaped shadow stepped between their two cells. It was Detective Riley.

"How long have you been listening?" Bishop asked, narrowing his eyes.

"Long enough." Detective Riley answered from the hall.

Sir Alfred asked calmly, "What do you mean 'better than the very thing itself'?"

When Detective Riley spoke again, his voice had lost something of the self-assuredness and bravado from before. Now it was tinged with humility. "The Bomb Squad is at Freemont's shop right now on orders of the Royal British Army. They're going to detonate the, what did you call it, *wormhole*?"

Bishop leapt up in his cell and pounded on the door wildly. "Detonate it? They can't do that!" He bounced around like a caged animal.

Detective Riley stepped closer to the door and asked, with all sincerity, "Why? What will happen?"

"What *wouldn't* happen? Look around you, fool! Look at what is already happening! Multiply that times a thousand! Times a billion!" Bishop hollered.

Detective Riley squatted down to be at the same eye level as the slot openings in both the cell doors.
Sir Alfred and Bishop were now able to see his face, which, they noticed, was no longer stiff and stubborn-looking. "Gentlemen, explain to me what is happening down in that cellar. Help me to do the right thing."

After a long pause, Sir Alfred called out to Bishop. "For the sake of all we've worked to protect, Bishop, Keeper my Keeper, tell him only what you must."

Frustrated, Bishop began with insults. "For starters, that THING you commandeered so ignorantly and then turned over to the military like a complete MORON is—"

"Bishop," interrupted Sir Alfred, reminding him to get to the point.

"Fine. That *thing* is not capable of being destroyed. If it were, then it would have been done eons ago by people much smarter than those who dare toy with it now."

"So what will bombing it do?" asked Detective Riley.

Bishop snorted a laugh just to keep from screaming.

"Calm, Bishop. Calm," Sir Alfred intoned, but he didn't feel calm, either.

"The question is almost as preposterous as the result," Bishop went on. "The greatest astrophysicists on the planet couldn't describe such a catastrophe accurately. They could only guess at what might happen."

Detective Riley cajoled him further, "You seem to be smart enough to give it a try."

"Very well. Exploding *it* would result in internal fragmentations to the nth degree – 'n' being equal to infinity."

"English, please."

Bishop was losing his patience, having to describe his worst nightmare as the clock counted down to its actually coming true. He raised his voice with exasperation at this feeble-minded civilian who had caused most of the trouble they were speaking of. "It will tear open ten times as many portals leading to ten times as many inexplicable dimensions in space and time, exposing ten times as many unforeseeable threats, as plants, animals, organisms and who-knows-what all mix into each others' planes of existence! Spillage, sir! SPILLAGE of epic proportions! Does that clear things up for you?" Bishop took a breath. "And what of it? What's a fool like you going to do about any of it?"

Detective Riley took no offense at Bishop's tirade. Instead, he was curious to know more. "Where is it from? How was it made?"

Sir Alfred's gentle tone seeped out from his cell, "You know in your heart that you do not need those answers to do what is right."

Detective Riley had always done what was 'right' in his career, he thought. He'd always followed orders. He'd given orders. All based on what the law told him was right. And where had it gotten him? He felt a new emotion rise up in him that he didn't quite recognize. *It's time I decide for myself what's right*, Riley thought.

He turned a key in the slot of the first cell door to reveal the grateful face of Sir Alfred. Detective Riley then proceeded to do the same to Bishop's door, only this time the door opened to reveal...

PEPPER SPRAY!!!

"Ahhh!" Riley screamed as the burning sensation blinded his eyes.

Bishop stepped out with his chest puffed as Petey scurried to retrieve his family tree scroll from Sir Alfred's hand. Bishop shrugged his shoulders at an incredulous Sir Alfred and placed Petey back on his shoulder. "That was for being so stupid, Detective."

His eyes still watering and stinging, Detective Riley straightened up and stood face-to-face with the belligerent Bishop. The two men looked like boxers squaring off before the bell, only one was short and square, and the other old and smug.

Sir Alfred cleared his throat. "Men, we have much bigger fish to fry."

Reluctantly, Bishop and Detective Riley stood down. Just as they realized they shared a common goal, a blinding white flash lit the hallway unnaturally.

"What was..." Bishop started—
but he didn't have time to finish.

BOOM!

The entire building was rocked by an enormous sonic boom, knocking all three men to the floor violently. Slowly they recovered their senses before hearing sirens wailing all over the city. The three men shared a terrified look.

"We're too late," said Bishop, "They've detonated the rift."

TWENTY-FIVE

The Bubbling Springs

It had been a long, cold journey from their last stop in the abandoned mill, and Freemont's ankles were swollen and throbbing. He hadn't walked without the aid of his trusty cane for decades. But one thing did give him comfort. It was knowing that Julian was far away from the dangers of this place, back in London and safe in the care of his trusted Keepers by now.

Or so he thought.

Thump, drag.

Gabriel led him farther toward his lair by the glow of the thousand obedient firefly slaves that now enveloped their master like a king's robe.

They arrived at the base of a vast archipelago of volcanoes. There, in a rocky grotto, a shallow bed of water was heated by nearby lava, forming a most uninviting bubble bath.

"Ah, the Bubbling Springs," Gabriel grinned.

“And what are we doing here?” asked Freemont, expecting the worst.

“We are going to do a bit of relaxing,” answered Gabriel, “And by we, I mean...you.” He kicked the side of Freemont’s bad leg causing the old man to fall like a sack of potatoes onto the ashy rock of the grotto floor.

Once Freemont was down, Gabriel pricked a vein in his forearm with the end of a reed freshly plucked from the spring. Gabriel allowed its warm, bubbly elixir to rush directly into Freemont’s bloodstream.

Freemont was instantly lulled into a state of semi-consciousness.

Gabriel cackled proudly and addressed his minion fireflies like little beloved pets: his Children of the Night, “You see, my children? All I must do is trick his mind into thinking his body is already dead. Then it will have no reason to keep its steel trap shut any longer.”

Freemont hadn’t the time, or energy, to fight back. In fact, he actually welcomed this strange sensation that removed all of his pain.

“Wonderful feeling, isn’t it?” Gabriel asked, standing over Freemont’s listless body.

By now, Freemont could little understand the nuance of Gabriel’s words.

“The chemicals from the spring are lulling your body into a state of hibernation. Soon, your mind will think you are dead." Strangely, Gabriel's sweaty face displayed a bittersweet smile as he watched his father slip further into a coma-like condition.

He knelt down and stroked Freemont's meaty hand. "I wish things had gone differently, father. I wish you could have found a way to love me for who I am. A man born with ambition. A man born to lead." In the corner of Gabriel's colorless eye, he felt a sudden sting from where a tear wanted to form, but instead only dryness scratched at it like sandpaper.

Freemont imagined himself shaking his head back and forth, but he lacked the strength to make it so. A single word trickled faintly from Freemont's old bluing lips, "Curse."

"Yes," sympathized Gabriel, "It is a curse to be burdened with so powerful a secret."

Freemont's mouth moved but Gabriel could not hear any more. He leaned in closer.

Freemont finished, "Curse…dies…with me."

Gabriel's face turned stone cold. He stood up in a fit of rage, pushed a large rock into the bubbling spring, splashing boiling water everywhere. He screamed with frustration. The rocky grotto amplified Gabriel's voice and launched into the air, where it gained the attention of a black beast, flying overhead. The beast – a large pterodactyl-sized bat – was screeching in pain.

Gabriel recognized his scout. He watched as it flew haphazardly toward the master it had been seeking. The bat crash-landed on its back just outside the grotto where Gabriel remained standing over Freemont.

Gabriel could see that his servant had been speared through the heart and was now dying.

This was one more frustration that further enraged Gabriel. "Who in the realm dares kill my scout?" he shouted to the sky.

He approached the creature, carefully avoiding the black blood that spurted from its chest with every pulse. Upon closer inspection, Gabriel discovered that the spear was actually Freemont's cane – the one that had been left back in the clock shop. Gabriel's eyes narrowed with suspicion. "Monty?" he asked quizzically, "How is it that your cane found its way across dimensions of time and space and into my scout's belly?"

ZZZZZZZZZZZZZZZZZ.

"Perhaps I could answer that for you, darling."

Gabriel heard the refined female voice buzz by his face and turned to find its owner. "Who speaks to me now?"

The Lady in Red curtsied in the air before the Dark One, batting her long eyelashes. "Just a lady who rather enjoys Delphisola the way it is. Who wants to age, anyway?" she cooed with a very practiced giggle.

"Speak, bug. I am in no mood," barked Gabriel.

"Well, if it's a bother, then I suppose I won't say that I saw the youngling who brought that cane to this island."

"Youngling?"

"Yes. A creature of your kind, darling. Only half-sized. Julian, his friends called him."

Freemont's eyes suddenly opened! *JULIAN!* he panicked, *Here in this dimension?* It was all Freemont could do to keep his mind focused on their conversation, despite it becoming fainter by the moment.

Gabriel considered the ladybug's story then shifted his eyes to Freemont, "Julian? Is that one of your new Keepers, Monty? Sent to save you, old chap?" Gabriel bent over Freemont and looked into his glassy eyes. "Can you hear me in there? This Julian must care very deeply about you to risk his life by coming here. And I reckon a person who cares that deeply about you is someone you care equally for, wouldn't you say?"

Freemont's pupils dilated just enough to display the fear growing inside him...
No!

Gabriel sucked his teeth and stepped back over to the slain beast as it gurgled blood and choked on its last breath. "But why would your 'hero' bring you your cane? Unless..."
Gabriel dug his boot into the beast's neck for leverage and pulled the cane out from its belly. "Unless...it has some sort of significance to you? Some instrument you hope to defeat me with? I mean, certainly this could not be..." His smile faltered. He repeated with even greater disbelief, "It *couldn't* be!"

He thought back to when he had first attacked Freemont at the clock shop. He recalled how the cane was the very first thing Freemont had reached for, and the only thing he'd ever kept by his side – for decades!

"Of course!" The wind was nearly knocked from Gabriel's sails as the profundity of his discovery swept over him. He cackled his most sinister and long lasting laugh yet. "This? This is the Sacred Object you've been protecting all these years?"

He wielded the cane with renewed confidence. "Why, you clever man. What is it? Something in its golden handle? Some material hidden inside the little doves, perhaps?" Gabriel strolled about the rocky terrain with a sudden calm. "How convenient that for all these years it was right by your side in your greedy little clutches." He combed back his greasy hair with the tips of his fingers and looked upon his island with invigorated eyes. "And now look. It's been delivered right to me. Oh, the irony is just too much to take."

Gabriel swung the cane toward the post-ecliptic moons, all fully relit, above. "Oh, dark sky, how I can't wait to tear a new rift into your skin to return home with the Sacred Object and fulfill my destiny as the true Father."

But the echoing return of his voice was quietly outlasted by the soft, breathy laugh of an increasingly delirious Freemont. The old man was now fully overtaken by the chemicals. They loosened his tongue and unlocked his protective mind.

Gabriel turned around and observed Freemont's pathetic little laughter with great curiosity. "You've finally gone mad, old man? Good. One more trait we will share."

Freemont mustered up just enough energy to whisper, "You...are...still...blind." He pushed the words out like puffs of air.

Gabriel intentionally flashed his colorless eyes so that Freemont could see what this dimension has done to them. “The product of living in the dark, compliments of you.”

Freemont’s now completely unlocked mind allowed his secrets to flow from his mouth like water from an open floodgate, “That cane is but a stick to help me walk, you fool. The Sacred Object is not a piece of wood. ‘Tis a piece of me.”

“What do you mean that it’s a piece of you? Is the Sacred Object a piece of your heart? Is that why your heart is weakened? Tell me. Give what you owe to me now!”

Freemont’s memory flashed again to the catastrophic explosion during the Second Great Battle. He saw himself on his knees on the barren plateau, devastated. Gone was the loving young couple that had been taken by the ripple. Gone, too, was the young Gabriel he had banished into the rift.

But what was left in that moment was what Freemont fought to protect - the small wooden box bearing the Keepers’ insignia.

The young Freemont took the tip of his cane and inserted it into the insignia on the wooden box and, with a twist, unlocked it to reveal much more than any ‘object’ hidden inside. There was no keeping it secret anymore.

Back in the grotto, the helpless old man whispered to Gabriel, “That box that you struck so many years ago was no ordinary box. It was a basket that cradled a beautiful newborn baby - the son of your twin brother Allister."

Gabriel collapsed to the ashen rock of the grotto floor. "Allister had a son?" he asked softly, sincerely. "My brother had a child and no one told me about it?"

"Now, my son...you know all. The very brother you condemned had inherited the gift of power you had always wanted - in his heart - and he passed that power on to the heart of his firstborn, Julian." Freemont added, "This is why Allister distanced himself from you – to protect everyone from your greed, even you. He had no choice. The power of the Sacred Object was in Allister's blood as my firstborn, passed to the blood of his own firstborn."

Gabriel could not believe what he was hearing. "Allister? Your firstborn? We were twins for God's sake. Born less than a minute apart!"

"An eternity in your case, Gabriel. It appears, my son, that you have always been at odds with time."

There was nothing Gabriel despised more than being compared to his precious brother, Allister.

"I'm sorry, Gabriel. But it was never in your destiny."

Gabriel stormed out of the grotto and stood over the far edge, staring into the Lakes of

Fire before his volcanic lair. He snapped Freemont's antique cane in half over his knee and tossed the pieces into the bubbling spring. "Not in my destiny, you say?"

His icy eyes searched the landscape of Delphisola like two hawks dispatched into the night. It was time he met this Julian, in person. "Well… let's see if my destiny can be rewritten."

TWENTY-SIX

The Third Great Battle Begins

Gabriel basked in the warmth of his firefly robe, utterly unconcerned for Freemont, who lay helpless, trussed up in a tree within the grotto, overlooking the sulfurous Bubbling Springs.

Gabriel scanned the stars as he contemplated his attack on the boy who dared to pursue him. One constellation suddenly rearranged itself into the shape of a mop-haired boy with funny front teeth. Gabriel seethed, "Julian."

The constellation then expanded, changing the boy's image into a grown man's which spanned the entire sky until it finally disappeared, giving way to something familiar raging straight toward him. It was his very own dimension-hopping aircraft!

The Black Taxi cut through the sky smoothly. Whoever piloted it was clearly more skilled than he had been at the controls, Gabriel thought. Normally this observation would bruise Gabriel's fragile ego, but today this was good news.

Could it really be that the Sacred Object was delivering itself right to him, like some holiday goose that cooked itself and climbed right onto his plate? Gabriel's colorless eyes, useless in his native world, were as sharp as a hawk's in this adopted dark homeland. Even from a hundred feet below, his eyes were able to zoom in on the craft, inside its open window and straight to the passenger seat, where he spotted not only the familiar curly brown hair passed down from his precious brother Allister, but also another signature family trait: that crooked Rigby lip.

Gabriel delighted in this evidence. *It is* ***him***, he thought.

A short distance away, the Black Taxi landed expertly on the ashen plateau that separated the Lakes of Fire from the Bubbling Springs. Lily, Martin and then Julian filed out, emboldened by their flight.

From across the plateau, Martin looked at the dreadful Gabriel, while standing protectively in front of Julian. "Mr. Dark One, it appears you are outnumbered," he shouted, like a Hollywood action hero.

Lily sighed. "From now on, let me do the talking," she hissed under her breath.

Martin shrugged, figuring the line was as good as any.

Uninterested in these two superfluous children, Gabriel craned his neck to get a better look at the one they guarded. "You must be Julian." He sneered.

From Julian's shirt pocket, Wilfred the Caterpillar peeked out, eyes squinting. "Careful, Mr. Julian. The Dark One cannot be trusted."

Julian refused to give Gabriel the satisfaction of a reply. Then something caught his attention. It was Granddad, strung up in a tree over a bubbling spring. He looked weak, tired and barely conscious.

Julian, filled with hope, worry, love and loss, rushed to the old man as fast as he could and began to untie him. "Granddad!"

Gabriel was content to merely observe the boy, at first. He wasn't sure just how powerful the Sacred Object was and, thus, calculated his next move.

Soon, Freemont was safely back on solid ground.

Julian gazed at his grandfather lovingly. "Say something, Granddad." Desperately, Julian placed Granddad's head gently on his lap and peered into his heavy eyes searching for recognition. Freemont's face, now more tired than ever, seemed to hide even more awful stories in the lines of each wrinkle.

Wilfred shook his tiny head, "I am so sorry, Mr. Freemont, for my role in this."

Julian turned with a most devastated look to his friends. "He's dying!"

Gabriel carefully took a step toward them, bringing with him the glow of a thousand obedient, writhing firefly slaves. "Yes, pity. I can honestly say that I tried...*everything.*"

Julian glared at Gabriel, who was momentarily quiet. He was mindful of the power of the Sacred Object and thus, quite mindful of the boy.

Lily and Martin approached Julian on both sides, keeping a close watch on Gabriel.

"We need to get him home, to the Keepers," Lily said. "They'll know how to help."

Gabriel snorted, "Yes, by all means. Go consult with those brave men who send children to do their bidding."

Julian gently lifted Granddad's head off his lap and stood tall. He glared at Gabriel menacingly from across the plateau. "Who does this to an old man?" Julian cried out at the smirking Gabriel, who stepped closer with each moment of inaction from the boy.

Why doesn't the Sacred Object flex his muscle? Gabriel wondered. Gabriel took great pleasure in recognizing his brother's traits, and even his own, in Julian's face, as they squared off like gunslingers about to duel.

But what the boy said next he found most intriguing of all. "What did my granddad ever do to you?"

Suddenly, Gabriel felt alive with promise. "Dear boy, do you know nothing of your granddad? Of me? Of...*you*?"

Julian felt as if he had been nailed to the ground. Of all the people he'd never truly known in his life, perhaps Julian Rigby was the one that he least understood. He looked to Lily and Martin, who waited for any command to attack this foul man they stood before.

Gabriel's dirty boot took one more step, giving his menacing shadow permission to encroach upon Julian's space. "It seems we have both been kept in the dark for too long, boy. Stay with me, Julian, and I shall answer all your questions and more."

Freemont let out an unintelligible sound, but even that was more than he could afford.

Martin knelt down by the old man, clocking his weakening pulse.

Julian quickly rejected Gabriel's offer. "I have no questions for you."

"Nonsense. You are filled with questions. I can feel them in you. And I have all the answers."

"No more than the lies of a madman, I'm sure," Wilfred shouted from Julian's pocket.

Gabriel detested how freely the Keepers labeled him mad. *Is it madness to lead when you know it to be your destiny? Is it madness to expect your own blood to love and support you?* "Who is that you have with you, boy? My little Wilfred?"

Wilfred shivered with fear and slid back down into Julian's pocket, hiding.

Gabriel chuckled, "I thought I ended his miserable little life, you know, out of pity." Gabriel whispered something to his firefly slaves, and a wave of flickering light undulated through their collective shape as if they were sending a signal to... someone.

Julian stepped back. "We are leaving now. With Granddad."

"Oh, I think not." And with that, Gabriel lifted a grimy horn to his lips and sounded a blast so ugly and so shatteringly loud that all three friends clasped their hands to their ears in pain.

Gabriel's dark army emerged from behind every shadow, crevice and cavern of the ashen rock plateau. They hopped, wriggled, slithered and limped. All manner of nocturnal creatures - mangy felines, vampire bats, owls that appeared and disappeared at will, red-eyed wolves, scorpions the size of dinner plates, black widow spiders, a swarm of night locusts and much more. These were his Children of the Night.

Cloaked in fireflies and backed by a most horrible army, Gabriel stepped forward once more. "What were you thinking? That you would enter my dominion, invade my lair and simply…take, from *me*?"

Julian's heart fell a thousand feet within in his chest. "Isn't that what you've done to me?" he asked, trying to mask the fear in his voice as best he could.

Gabriel smiled at the attempt, "That depends on where you start the story, child."

Martin and Lily stood close to Julian over Freemont's listless body as the Dark Army encroached.

"We've got to do something, Rigby!" Martin said, as he held Lily protectively.

"Boil the old man and the others in the lakes, and bring me the scrawny boy," Gabriel commanded.

"No!" Lily screamed. But before anyone could make a move, a deafening croak suddenly shook the ashen plateau like thunder.

Gabriel turned to see a huge, rolling dark fog in the distance tumbling toward them. From inside the fog came the rhythm of a familiar female voice. "Boyyyyy?" the voice questioned. Then, after a long and drawn-out breath came…"I see no boyyyyy here."

The fog having cleared, Pythia was revealed seated atop her granite pedestal that was now carried like a canopy on the porcelain-like shoulders of a one-thousand-strong fairy army, their bodies glowing defiantly bright to spite the Dark One.

The more the mysterious fog unfolded, the more and more members of the Rebel Army came into view. Pythia had amassed creatures from all across the realm, both familiar and new to Julian and the others.

Flanking each side of the army were the Whistling Winds of the Desert, wielding sound as their sword. Their high-pitched battle cries shrieked at Gabriel in unison.

Even the single black crow that had followed Julian everywhere flew over the rebels as their eye-in-the-sky.

Then Julian saw a most unexpected and welcome sight on the horizon…a fleet of ships sailing safely atop the Lakes of Fire. A closer look revealed that the ships were carrying the united tribes of the Enchanted Forest and were actually not ships at all – they were long, sturdy, black-barked trunks of the Weeping Willows.

Martin turned joyfully to Julian, "It appears you have more friends than you thought."

Gabriel was seething. "A frog that dares not leap, trees who weep all the night and fairies no longer fit to fly. Is this truly all the glory you have to offer me? Defeating a band of misfits?"

Gabriel's minions sneered and laughed at their leader's musings.

Pythia drew a long breath, then exhaled, "Fear us. Or fear us nooooot. It makes no difference. Your fate is sealed. And your dessssstiny has been seeeeeen."

Gabriel and his dark army stood united on one side of the ashen plateau.

Pythia and her ragtag rebels stood firmly on the other.

Between them were a boy, his loyal friends, a pet caterpillar and a dying old man.

"As your ruler, I will offer amnesty only once," Gabriel shouted at the Rebel Army. "Turn back now and you will live – stay, and you shall all die."

Pythia and the rebels showed no sign of retreat. Pythia drew another long breath and released a melodic response, "Noooo, Dark One, we shall die no moooore for you." Then she opened her large mouth in what Gabriel expected to be her typical lethargic yawn.

Instead, her long sticky tongue unrolled and sprung out at Gabriel like a lightning-fast whip. In a second, his entire robe of firefly slaves had been snatched away. Their light and their lives were extinguished in a flash as Pythia recoiled her tongue.

CRUNCH.

Pythia slowly chewed his little pets. "The emperor wears nooooo robe," she exhaled with a smile.

Gabriel's blood boiled hotter than the water of the Bubbling Springs, hotter than the lava of the nearby Lakes of Fire that bordered their battleground.

Hotter than the suns that had abandoned this realm when he arrived.

"War it is, then," he snarled.

TWENTY-SEVEN

An Island at War

"Warriors of the night, your thirst for blood shall now be quenched!" Gabriel surveyed his dark army that covered the ashen plateau behind him, and smiled. "I promised that I would make this island yours, and today I deliver on that promise."

The Dark Army roared a thunderous battle cry.

"Now go! Feast on the flesh of your enemies!"

The two armies came together in an inevitable clash of darkness and light. Julian, Lily and Martin shielded Freemont's feeble, old body as they watched in terror.

The thick, rolling fog thunder-clapped from the north side of the plateau. With a vengeance, it tumbled over Gabriel's warriors, temporarily half-blinding them.

Flanking the sides of the Dark Army, the Whistling Winds screamed in frequencies so shrill that Javelinas threw themselves on the ground, whimpering like wounded puppies.

Julian held tight to Granddad as a maelstrom of fog and ash whirled around them. He tried to block out the horrible sounds of gnashing teeth, ferocious growls and clanging battle sticks but they were too loud to ignore.

Across the battlefield, Pythia slowly stepped from her pedestal, touching the ground for the first time since *He* had come to her land. She set her bulging eyes on Gabriel. No longer a slave to the toxins she had breathed for over a decade, Pythia crept more steadily now. More like a panther than a frog, she stalked her prey.

With furious lashes of his bullwhip, Gabriel cut through the battlefield. Then something caught his attention. His rage-crazed eyes locked on Pythia's.

The two enemies came within twenty feet of each other, and then stopped. Gabriel was but a fraction of Pythia's size, but she knew better than to underestimate him.

He, on the other hand, did not. "Once I destroy the great Seer, who shall be left to falsely predict the future, as you've done for so long?"

Pythia crouched down lower, leaning back on her massive hind legs. "But I foretold of your defeat, Dark One, and here we staaaand," she replied.

Gabriel made his bullwhip gracefully twirl on the ashen soil, kicking up a whirl of dust around it. Snakelike, it seemed to dance inside the dust. As if hypnotic, it lulled Pythia into a sort of trance.

Gabriel smiled, clearly enjoying the effect his whip had on his enemy. "Oh pitiful toad, you don't really think you have what it takes to leap after so many years?"

Determinedly, Pythia broke her gaze from the whip and returned it to Gabriel. "Time to find out!" She bellowed a thunderous croak and leapt at him with all her might.

Her shadow darkening all but his white eyes, Gabriel flicked his wrist and released his obedient whip, sending it flying into the air.

Pythia had no time to grasp what was coming next. The leathery strand came to life in flight and became a vicious serpent that took the great frog by surprise and coiled itself around her rubbery body with an iron grip. By the time she landed at Gabriel's feet with a thump, her lungs had already been crushed.

Gabriel watched as Pythia gasped for air. "Oh, to be back on your pedestal, eh, frog? I bet a sweet breath of toxic gas would hit the spot right now." He couldn't help but snicker as his serpent loosened its hold around Pythia and slithered obediently back to him. "Tell me, Oracle, did you *see* that one coming?"

"Get back, you furry creeps!" Lily gave a flying roundhouse kick to the slobbering Javelinas nipping at her and her friends. A side kick. A throat strike. All sorts of well-practiced maneuvers. But still, it wasn't enough.

The Dark Army was too strong; Javelinas were closing in on her and Martin from all sides; Freemont's heartbeat was getting slower and weaker, and Julian was starting to wonder how much longer the old man could last.

Suddenly, a blurry mist descended upon them and everything went a dark, smoky grey.

"Lily?!" Julian looked around, terrified.

"Julian!" Martin shouted through the muffled fog.

Fog, that's what it was. The dark fog had swept up and engulfed the friends so quickly, none saw it coming.

On the other side of the foggy wall, Javelinas snorted and drooled in confusion. Where was their quarry? Quick as a whisper, the fog traveled away, wafting over the molten Lakes of Fire.

What the Javelinas couldn't see - much less comprehend - was that their prey was now sitting comfortably on the nubby trunk of a great willow tree that had now been sailing inside that fog atop the lava.

"Pleased to see you again...*boys*," said a familiar booming voice.

And Lily couldn't have been happier to hear it, even if it did refer to her as a boy. "Bogford!" Lily shouted and patted his bark gratefully. "I told you that the Willows would one day be guardians again. My valiant knight!"

Greetings exchanged, the friends looked into the fog trying to determine for whence they were bound.

"Do you feel that?" Julian asked, reaching down to touch his sneaker. "It's hot down there!"

A fiery glow lit up beneath the friends and their makeshift tree-raft savior.

"Where are we?" Martin asked, somewhat taken aback by the sight.

"We are sailing the Lakes of Fire. I'm taking you back to your flying machine," Bogford shouted assuredly over the din.

Seconds later, the grey, misty fog around them lifted on one side, revealing that they had sailed to the other end of the vast plateau and had arrived at the landing site of the Black Taxi.

Using his free branches, Bogford lifted them all gently to solid ground. The friends were exhausted but grateful. Martin, displaying the strength of a man twice his size, did his best to support Freemont over his shoulder.

"Well done, Sir Martin," commented Bogford as he kept watch along with the fog that continued to hide the friends from the Dark Army's view.

Moments later, inside the Black Taxi - with Lily safely in the back seat and Freemont lying comfortably beside him - Martin turned the key to the ignition.

VROOM!

That wonderful sound meant one thing to all of them: freedom!

But it meant quite another to Gabriel, still in pursuit.

Martin turned to Julian, who stood guard outside the taxi. "Climb in!"

As Julian stepped closer to do just that, the wall of fog that had surrounded and protected the friends for so long was blown away as if by a tornado. The rush of wind also caused Julian to stumble back and fall to the ground.

Lily pointed up in terror. "What's that?"

A flock of Gabriel's giant bats zeroed in on the Black Taxi. It was now obvious that it was the fluttering of their wings that had blown back the protective fog.

No longer hidden by the fog, Gabriel spotted them from across the plateau. "Destroy them!"

"Julian!" Lily screamed.

WHACK WHACK WHACK SCREECH!

Suddenly, the bats set upon the Black Taxi in a deafening hail of terror.

"Julian, get in the car!" Martin shouted.

"Come on, Julian! Get in!" cried Lily.

But it was too late. The car was lifted into the air just as the engine sprang to life. Its wheels spun uselessly as the grip of the bats' gnarly feet raised the taxi higher. The rapidly changing view of Julian made him look smaller and smaller.

"Martin, we can't leave Julian! Do something!" Lily screamed. But suddenly Lily's eyes widened as she locked onto Martin's terrified gaze.

"Are we now—?" began Martin.

"—Falling!" Lily shouted.

Gabriel curled his upper lip with delight at the fate of the Black Taxi's inhabitants, then he scanned the battleground once more – searching for the thing he desired more than life itself…the Sacred Object.

"Lily! Martin!" Julian shouted frantically over the ledge of the plateau where his friends had just fallen in the Black Taxi.

A muffled shout arose from the steam. *Was that Martin?* Julian wondered.

The fog returned and encircled Julian once more. But it was no use. Gabriel had already discovered the boy's whereabouts.

Julian suddenly clasped his chest in pain. His heart ached. Was he having a heart attack? Here? Now? "Granddad?" Julian whispered.

This was no heart attack. This was something Julian couldn't quite name. The memory of Granddad's voice played in his mind. "Our hearts are like a clock, Julian. Never should they be allowed to stop ticking."

Suddenly Julian's memory was interrupted by the sound of footsteps.

Thump, drag.

Thump, drag.

"Granddad? Is that you?" Julian peered into the fog still surrounding him.

The footsteps stopped.

The fog could not protect him any longer.

Thump, drag.

Inside Julian's pocket, Wilfred's little hairs all stood up on his back.

Gabriel entered the inner ring of whirling mist. He smiled at the boy. For the first time, they were face-to-face. "Finally, I get to meet you. I've heard such good things."

TWENTY-EIGHT

Fire and Fog

What Gabriel didn't know when the Black Taxi had earlier plummeted over the cliff and headed straight toward the boiling lava, was that the taxi had come to a sudden, jolting, and very complete stop.

"What was that? What happened? Are we dead?" Lily asked, looking around wildly.

Martin peered out the windshield and pointed. "Not dead. Just dangling above a lake of fire."

Incredibly, the Black Taxi had landed on a ledge that jutted out over the molten rock. As if to punctuate that terrible fact, the taxi slid forward a few inches, sending rocks and gravel down into the lava, where they melted immediately.

"Martin, let's go!" Lily shouted.

Martin pressed the accelerator once more and the car roared – but only for a second. A knocking noise from under the hood rattled loudly. The engine sputtered and gave out.

"Not the timing belt again!" cried out Lily.

Martin put his hand to Freemont's chest. It was just as he thought. The ticking of his heart had slowed even more. "He's not going to make it, Lily. We have to find Julian. We have to get back home."

But Julian was otherwise occupied. Gabriel stepped menacingly closer to the boy, who had stumbled back until he found himself against a rock wall. Julian was repulsed by what he took in. Not just by Gabriel's odor but by everything from his near translucent skin to his long and dark hair, thick with grease...and his soulless eyes. They, perhaps, were the worst.

Gabriel unlocked the buckle on his flight suit and caressed his beloved bullwhip once more. "I would like to think you'd come willingly with me, Julian. But at this point in our relationship, I just see that as...well, unlikely." Gabriel's white eyes stared greedily down at the boy like a thief just about to steal a golden treasure.

Julian could still feel Granddad's pain, and his own heart could not find a steady rhythm. It skipped a beat. Two. Three. It added beats where none should have been. *What is happening to me?* he thought, *And where are my friends?*

Once again, Gabriel made his bullwhip dance in the soil, just as he had when he attacked Pythia, and once again, the graceful movement of the bullwhip began to lull its victim. With a satisfied smile, Gabriel released the whip, sending the uncoiling serpent straight toward Julian.

Julian gasped for air as the whip-snake wound itself around his throat, beginning to choke the life out of him. Then, suddenly, the serpent squeaked, and fully released its grip on the boy. *What could be happening now?* Julian wondered faintly.

The snake was met by not one, but two, three, then four other serpents - only golden, braided serpents – in full attack mode.

Julian's eyes traced the golden strands back to their source. He was too shocked to smile, even in relief, when he saw that the braids were attached to the head of someone very welcome indeed. The braids were those once wrapped so neatly, like a turban, atop the head of Florinia. He was saved again.

Florinia nodded at Julian then whipped her neck around so quickly that her braids flung Gabriel's serpent back to the edge of the plateau.

The serpent landed as lifeless and leathery as it was as a bullwhip.

"Hey, that can be our timing belt!"

Shocked to hear Lily's voice, Julian turned to see her clambering up and over the cliff's edge and back onto the plateau, looking worse for the wear.

"Lily?" Julian called out.

Gabriel's voice meanwhile did not conceal his sarcasm. "Really? A fairy? Do you think that's a fair fight?" Gabriel sneered at Florinia and the glowing white, defiant light that surrounded her.

Gabriel ached to kill Florinia. He fixed his murderous eyes on the glowing fairy and considered his options, missing a small but very significant action.

Quick as a flash, Lily plucked Gabriel's leathery bullwhip from the ground and turned with it to disappear back over the cliff.

"I've wanted to take you on for a long time, Dark One," Florinia taunted.

Gabriel grinned. "How nice for you, fairy, that your dying wish will come true."

Florinia stood protectively in front of Julian. Gabriel's milky eyes glared at the boy then flicked back to the impudent fairy.

Taking care of Florinia shouldn't take long, he decided. Gabriel gestured behind him.

"Do you hear that? My army is trouncing your pitiful rebels as we speak, Florinia. Your forest friends will retreat without you, and soon my warriors will be pulling your feathers from their teeth."

Florinia knew the Dark One was right. She could hear it in the increasingly desperate sounds of the battle taking place outside the fog. But she would not leave the boy. She owed him that much.

Over the din of battle rose another sound. A coughing, choking, sputtering sound. Gabriel jerked his chin to the sky. He knew that sound.

"Told you it was the timing belt!" Lily shouted happily as Martin expertly steered the Black Taxi up and over the cliff. "Down there! He's with Florinia!" Lily exclaimed.

Despite everything, Julian found himself smiling for the first time in a long time. His friends were safe, and so was Granddad.

Martin steered the car a bit lower and tilted it just slightly to one side. Julian's heart lifted when he saw the window roll down, just a little, and the tired old face of his grandfather peer out at him.

With a shout of defeat, the rebel army began to scatter hopelessly. Julian looked around wildly, not sure what to do next. It was over. It was all coming to an end. Julian looked up at his beloved granddad.

As Freemont's eyes met Julian's, a single tear trickled down the old man's cheek. The tear traveled down the lines of Freemont's deepest wrinkles, collecting all the stories he had hidden and never told. The tear grew bigger and bigger until it fell from his tender cheek, out the window of the taxi and down through the night sky of Delphisola like a lonely raindrop, until it dissolved in the cruel flames of the Lakes of Fire.

Martin shouted down at the rebel army, "Do not retreat! Don't leave him!"

But it was no use.

From within the arena of whirling fog below, Florinia messaged back up to Martin and Lily. Strangely, Julian heard it too. *Bring the old one home. We will protect the Savior.*

Lily and Martin looked toward each other. There was no way that Florinia could make good on that promise. It just seemed impossible.

Martin shook his head, "No chance."

A second message came into their minds; this time from Julian, *Saving Granddad was the mission. Go! Now!*

Down on the ground, the rebel army rapidly abandoning him, stood Julian.

Martin couldn't hold back his tears. "Negative, Rigby. We're not leaving without you!"

This time Julian cupped his hands and communicated the old-fashioned way, "Listen to me, for once!" he shouted over the din, "Take Granddad to the dry cleaner's! Go! Quickly!"

Martin turned again to Lily. "The dry cleaners? Who thinks about dry cleaning at a moment like this?"

Lily's eyes lit up. The Chronus Family Cleaners, of course, where the Keepers of Time hid their secret chamber. It made perfect sense. Besides, Lily knew that Julian was right. If they didn't get Freemont back home, he would be dead soon. She reached from the back seat to put her hand on the wheel and looked at Martin tenderly. "We have no choice."

Go. Do it for me, Julian sent the message as he looked up at his dear friends.

"NO!" Martin shouted into the fog but, reluctantly, he veered the craft away. As the Black Taxi rattled around them, Martin reached decidedly for one specific knob to press.

"How do you know it's that one?" shouted Lily over the whirring wind.

"Because it's the only one I don't know," he answered, eyes burning with tears. Suddenly, under the shimmer of the purple crescent moons, the Black Taxi dematerialized into nothingness, then – FLASH – a blinding white light lit the sky followed instantly by an accompanying supersonic boom.

In that moment, that fraction of immeasurable time, Delphisola had no shadows, no blackness, and no dark.

Back in London, down in the shadowy, secret chambers of the Keepers of Time, Linus shivered slightly. Slowly, very slowly, he opened his eyes and began to thaw from his frozen state.

While on Delphisola, just as quickly as it had come, the cosmic flash was gone - and with it, Julian's friends, his granddad, and his only ride home.

Florinia watched the sky intently. Legions of Gabriel's rabid bats were darkening the horizon forcing the fog to scatter, essentially abandoning its post.

Julian remained strangely calm. "Tell me something, Mr. Gabriel," he asked.

"Anything, boy."

"Why didn't you try to stop them? Your prisoner. My friends. You let them all leave with your craft. You didn't even *try* to stop them."

Gabriel nodded, containing his excitement.

Four of Gabriel's wolves had encircled Florinia, restraining her by her golden braids and allowing him to step as close as he wanted to the boy. He whispered with a malicious sincerity, “Because all I want is right here. And what’s here is infinitely more useful.” He reached for Julian’s wrist but, before he was able to get a solid grip on him, the boy was ripped away.

Julian could feel his body soar up into the sky. Or was it his soul? Some out-of-body experience?

The battleground got smaller and smaller beneath him as did a furious Gabriel, who cursed back up at the sky, “Noooooooooo!”

Florinia sent Julian a message from below, *Don’t be afraid, Julian. It has been seen!*

Julian was thoroughly confused. What manner of bird had plucked him from the danger below? He craned his neck to look and stared right into a blinding white glow. It took a moment for Julian’s eyes to adjust. This was no bird at all. It was a youngling.

“Hello again, Julian.”

“Eleazar?”

TWENTY-NINE

Julian's Flight

Eleazar gracefully swam the infinite sky like a dolphin while holding on to his new companion tightly beneath him.

For his part, Julian had his eyes clenched shut, hands in front of his face.

Eleazar messaged, *Feeling all right?*

Julian messaged back, *Not really! And anyway, I don't get it. How are you flying?*

Quite simple. I just jump on the wind's back and go, Eleazar answered coyly.

Yes, but your Feather of Fancy? I thought Gabriel took them from all the fairies!

The youngling fairy held steady his glide with his left wing and dipped the corner of his right down in front of Julian's face. *You mean this?*

Julian peaked through his fingers just enough to see it. A feather as fine as those he had seen bundled together inside the engine of the Black Taxi, covered with that same shimmering gold dust.

It's right where it's always been, finished Eleazar.

Julian was pleased to learn that at least one forest fairy still had his special feather, but couldn't understand how. *Gabriel hasn't taken it?* he messaged, keeping his hands clasped over his eyes tightly.

Eleazar flew purposefully through the night sky of a dark world. His young voice floated back down into Julian's mind. *The Dark One never knew I existed, Julian. Well, until now. You see, I was the only child fairy alive when He arrived and stopped time in our world. The tribe kept me hidden to protect the last of our kind. It is because of them that I am able to fly, and because of Him that I am unable to grow.*

Julian messaged the words he'd read in a book in Headmaster Benson's office but never quite believed for himself. *But...all children grow up.*

All except one, Eleazar responded with a laugh, as if there were a part of him inside that relished forever being a youngling. He then playfully spun Julian around in the night sky. *You might want to open your eyes now, Julian.*

Why would I do that?

So you can stop being afraid.

Julian absorbed these words now more than he ever did those from all the others who had spoken them before. *Easier said than done.*

"Whooo-hoooo!" suddenly cried a familiar little voice from Julian's pocket. It was Wilfred, still clinging on, and he had never been so happy in all his life. "He's right, Julian. It's breathtaking. The most beautiful thing I have ever seen." The little caterpillar did not need his glasses to see and feel what was happening. Tears streamed down his happy, little face.

Eleazar breathed in the night air. He so enjoyed the rushing wind on his skin. These flights had been so few and far between for him. *I, too, used to live in fear. It robbed me of flights like this one. It stole my youth, despite appearances. And it made me betray someone very special.*

Though flying at an incredible speed and altitude, his life in danger and all that, Julian thought, he felt a certain kindred spirit with both Eleazar and Wilfred. It was as if they were just three friends chatting on a patch of grass. But this was no patch of grass. Julian was soaring through the night sky of a world that existed in another plane outside of what he thought reality was.

One by one, Julian nervously loosened his fingers and opened his eyes. After all he'd been through, what did he have to lose?

What met his eyes was a sight – no, a feeling, that he couldn't have imagined. There it was; a world dipped in black. And it wasn't scary. It was...*magical.* It was glorious. Amazing. He felt like Peter Pan flying through Neverland.

Eleazar pressed, *Well?*

Will is right! Exhilarating! He saw hues of purple and gold from the moons. Stars that sparkled like diamonds, constellations that changed positions and formed new playful ones for Julian's amusement. One formed a dove that flew alongside them. Another made the image of a grandfather clock, reminiscent of his family heirloom.

The three companions shot like comets across the sky encased by the glow of Eleazar's aura. *You see, Julian, why fear all that might go incredibly wrong...*He took Julian on a long arching swoop like a jet in an air show and then straight into the now cloud-like rolling fog that rose up to meet them. Then...

POOF!

Despite seeing only shades of grey, Julian could still hear Eleazar's voice in his head, *...when we can instead focus on all that might go incredibly right?*

Suddenly they came out the other side of the cloud and stopped in an empty part of the sky. *What do you mean, Eleazar? Where are you taking me?*

Eleazar now held Julian directly in front of him, and for the first time, he actually used spoken words. "To the Window in the Sky."

Julian's big brown eyes were bursting with hope. He whipped his head from side to side searching for the portal, but he saw nothing. "I don't see it."

"You're only choosing not to see it."

Julian did just as Bishop had once instructed him and focused his attention directly on the space before him. Only this time he was better at it. Slowly, the sky began to crackle. Electric blue lines raced this way and that over an oval shaped...*what? Could it be? Yes!* "The other end of the rift!" Julian was so excited he nearly lost his grip on Eleazar.

Eleazar smiled, "I discovered this during one of my secret flights after having watched a bird disappear in the sky. Naturally I thought it might be a Vanishing Owl, but we were up much too high."

Julian couldn't believe it. Granddad was already back home with Lily and Martin and now he was about to be there, too. Their mission would be a total success. He looked and saw the entire island in one quick glance.

Eleazar continued, "I flew to the exact spot where the bird had disappeared, but all that remained was a white feather floating, not falling, as if it were waiting - right there - for the rest of the bird to return. Then I felt a tugging sensation at the hem of my robe." Eleazar guided them further to demonstrate. The end of his tunic rose and pulled him toward the rift.

Julian asked, "Why did you not tell Gabriel so that he could leave your land?"

"Tell him what? That a fairy he did not know existed, used a power he did not allow? I could have been killed for either of those two crimes alone. Besides, by the time I found the window, he had already finished building his black flying machine. He could have left, and did, without any help from me."

Julian nodded understandingly.

Eleazar's eyes filled with regret. "I'm sorry I betrayed you, Julian. I was afraid."

Julian's face washed over with a similar shame, and so did Wilfred's. "I know the feeling."

Eleazar smiled. It was time to move on. "Now, let us return you to the land of Eng."

Julian furrowed his brow. "Excuse me?"

"Your friends said you were from the land of Eng. Eng-land?"

Julian laughed heartily, along with Eleazar and little Wilfred who asked, "Why are we laughing?"

They exchanged another fit of laughter, but then Julian's smile fell as sadness replaced his joy. "But what about Delphisola? Poor Pythia? Florinia? Your army?"

Eleazar reached out an open hand for Wilfred to climb aboard. It was Wilfred who answered, "Those are problems for Delphisolans to solve, Julian."

Eleazar added, "And in time, we will. But you must now think about your own tribe, waiting back home."

As difficult as it was going to be to leave new friends, especially those in need, Julian knew that they were right. His place was back on the other side of the rift, with Granddad and the clock shop.

Julian hugged the youngling fairy, and then turned to the little caterpillar. "You make a great pet."

Wilfred smiled, "And you a great man."

Julian approached the Window in the Sky with his hands stretched out before him. Instantly, he could feel the tugging sensation tickling the tips of his fingers. He turned back, "One more question."

Eleazar held Julian by his feet, preparing to guide him gently into the force of the rift. "Yes, Julian?"

"That white feather you found fluttering here in the sky. It didn't happen to be from a Mourning Dove, did it?"

"I do believe—" Eleazar stopped in mid-sentence, his mouth agape in terror. "Never mind! Go!" And with a final, more forceful push, Julian began to disappear into the rift.

Then, one of Gabriel's massive scouting bats slammed into the youngling fairy so hard that it sent him whirling off into the dark sky, and sent poor little Wilfred spiraling down into a free fall of his own.

Julian had not time to react. His hands were being pulled into the rift, then his head, then his body and legs – until something, or someone, suddenly jerked him backward several feet. Something had Julian's right leg in its grasp, and it was a grasp Julian was familiar with.

Gabriel grinned up malevolently at Julian. "I think I'm going to like this ride, boy!"

With a loud roar, the two disappeared into the rift. At the exact same moment, the Delphisolan sky sealed up again. The rift was nowhere to be seen.

A constellation of two warriors battling fiercely began to dance around the space where the rift had been.

THIRTY

Tick Tock

Outside Chronus Family Cleaners, Martin brought the Black Taxi to a stop and stared. "Lily, do you see this?"

The friends couldn't tear their gaze from the gaping hole in the wall of the humble store. A large blue drop cloth fluttered in the wind in a vain attempt to hide the area of destruction behind it.

From the back of the taxi, Lily anxiously looked at Martin. "There's no one here. Are you sure this is the one?"

Martin popped open the driver's door. "How many dry cleaners have a hole the size of this taxi blasted into their sides?"

"No time for cheekiness, Martin. We've got to get Freemont the help he needs before—" Lily was interrupted by the sight of a strange old man with soft, expressive eyes gazing mournfully at them from behind the fluttering drop cloth.

"We need help! Are you Bishop?" shouted Martin.

The man shook his head in the negative.

"Sir Alfred, then?"

Another shake. The man squinted to see who was in the passenger seat of the Black Taxi. He approached curiously and then noticed it was Freemont. Without a word, without another glance at Martin or Lily, he opened the passenger door.

"Who are you?" Martin pressed, glancing at Lily nervously.

It was Lily who realized it first, "Linus."

The man carefully scooped up his old friend.

Moments later, his face etched with worry, the still mute Linus ran warm water over a washcloth in the chipped bathroom sink and carried it to the back room of the store. There, Freemont was lying comfortably on a makeshift bed of plastic-wrapped, unclaimed dry cleaning.

"Good thing people forget their dry cleaning," Martin remarked nervously.

Lily asked, "Linus? Can you tell us what we should do?"

Linus didn't answer. Gently, he wiped the old man's brow with the washcloth and gazed down on his friend with great focus and compassion.

Freemont sighed and seemed to relax a little. But then his breath caught and he seemed, for a moment, not to be breathing at all.

"Please! Do something." Lily looked to Linus imploringly.

Linus could see the tenderness and concern in both Lily's and Martin's eyes. For the first time since the Black Taxi had arrived, and actually for the first time in quite a lot longer than that, Linus opened his mouth to speak. His voice was soft and emotional. "I cannot. His heart has been broken, again."

Martin stared at Linus quizzically. He didn't understand. "Heart attack?"

"I don't think that's what he meant, Martin," Lily chimed in, taking in the tender look in Linus' eyes as he wet his friend's brow again with the warm cloth.

Martin was baffled by Linus' remark. "Well, then what can heal a broken heart?"

Linus only shrugged dejectedly. "Only time. Our greatest friend – and greatest enemy."

Numbers, figures, shapes and crackling energy twisted themselves around Julian like whirling water as he traveled once again through the wormhole. Sights, sounds, colors and an incredible roar surrounded him completely. He felt dizzy and a little sick to his stomach. And he felt someone or something still gripping his leg!

With great effort, Julian forced his head down to see Gabriel's filthy fingerless leather glove reaching up from the funnel of imagery, locked onto his leg like a metal vise. Through space and time, they traversed together, connected like two links on the same chain. Gabriel moaned in what sounded to Julian like great pain.

Then Julian began to notice a pattern. Whenever they swung left or right in the tubular tunnel, Gabriel emitted another groan.

The rift. Gabriel was getting spaghettified! *How terrible for him*, Julian thought, and then he threw his weight from side to side toward the edges of the wormhole so that Gabriel would have an even rougher ride. With enough effort, Julian hoped he could shake him.

Gabriel began to scream and curse.

Too bad, thought Julian. *You shouldn't hitchhike, you know*. Julian threw his weight against another edge as hard as he could.

Gabriel let out a horrifying scream. Julian's plan had worked. The gloved hand slipped off his ankle and released the boy completely. Gabriel's screams echoed for a while until they disappeared into the whirling wash of light, sound and color.

Julian only had a moment to appreciate that his uninvited passenger was no longer with him when – WHUMP – he landed on his hands and knees in an enormous explosion of light. He closed his eyes to steady himself, took a deep breath, and then reopened his eyes. Blurrily, he could make out that he had landed in the cellar of his grandfather's clock shop.

Though Julian struggled with his vision because of the brightness of the passage, it was soon restored enough to allow something on the cellar floor to catch his eye. The riddle etched into the floor sharpened into focus before him. One sentence, in particular, stood out for Julian:

Trust in the shepherd, not the flock.

The words grabbed at Julian's heart. *Am I really the shepherd that Granddad spoke of?* He wanted to believe it. He would love to make true his mother's premonition that he was The One, just as he wished he could make the Oracle's prophecy regarding his being the Savior true.

But look how that turned out. Julian thought about how he had left behind the Delphisolans who had come to his defense...

broken, in defeat, and filled with disappointment.

Scattered all around the cellar, Julian saw his many silly gadgets and inventions. They seemed so irrelevant now. *And messy too,* he thought. He picked up a handful of gears then remembered...he hadn't left the cellar this way.

Suddenly, Julian's attention was snatched away from his gadgets by a slow, deliberate scraping sound coming from upstairs.

"Lily? Martin?" Excited to see his friends again - *And what friends I now know they are,* he thought, - Julian raced up the stairs to the clock shop.

But what he saw stopped him in his tracks. It wasn't Martin, nor was it Lily. From behind a tall shelf of clocks one aisle away, Julian caught sight of a man dressed only in a loincloth, his face painted a very bright blue and red.

This Aztec warrior, bedecked with a heavy obsidian necklace and lethal looking spear, stepped out from behind a bookshelf and glared at Julian.

Surprised, Julian took a step backwards which, must have invited an attack from the Aztec because the warrior suddenly glowered and raised his spear as if to throw it at Julian.

Without thinking, Julian whirled around and grabbed the disc-shaped Rigby Coat-of-Arms clock from the wall behind him and held it out like a knight using a shield for protection.

The boy and the warrior looked at each other with equal amounts of fear and shock, but the Aztec warrior's instincts were honed for battle.

The warrior lunged at Julian with his spear raised high. Julian cringed, ready to take a blow, but what happened next was unexpected. When the warrior's spear made contact with the Rigby Coat-of-Arms clock, the spear shattered to pieces. And not just a few pieces, but millions of pieces so small that they looked like dust!

Confused, Julian looked down at his new shield, and then back at his attacker, who stood completely dumbfounded. To Julian's utter surprise, a new look came over the Aztec's face. Carefully, he bowed his head at the boy with great respect.

"Uh, I'm not sure if you speak English, or maybe Spanish, but..." Julian took a small step back. He had to focus – how on earth did this man get into the clock shop, anyway? What was an Aztec warrior doing in London?

Julian didn't even have time to finish his thought. Rather, he set down the clock shield and, eyes wide; he turned toward the top of the cellar stairs. Someone – or something – was racing up those stairs. Julian swallowed his fear. “Sir Alfred? Bishop?”

What emerged from the cellar was most certainly not Sir Alfred or Bishop. No, it was a griffin that flew out of the cellar in a panic. Lost and obviously confused, the frightened beast began to lay waste to the clock shop.

“Stop! Wait!” There was nothing Julian could do. Besides, he wasn’t quite ready to take his eyes off the Aztec.

With its hard head, the griffin rammed the already damaged front door open. Immediately, the sounds of panic and confusion invaded the clock shop from outside. The griffin flew out the door and into the chaotic street.

Cautiously, Julian followed the creature’s path to the door. He stood rooted as he took in the mobbed streets outside in this normally quiet neighborhood. What on earth could be going on?

Then it hit Julian like a ton of bricks…*the rift*! Julian rushed down the cellar steps into the darkness below.

“Whoa!” Astonished, Julian saw where there had been one rift before, there were now ten, perhaps twelve new rifts taking shape one after the other. The portal had multiplied and created other portals to all kinds of worlds. Julian was horrified.

Out of one rift, a spectacular flock of shadow birds suddenly emerged. Manically searching for an escape, the shadows flew up the cellar stairs and into the clock shop, becoming more and more panicked, knocking more and more fragile clocks to the ground. Finally, the noise upstairs was gone and Julian knew they had escaped into the street.

Within seconds, Julian noticed a green slime pouring out from another of the rifts, climbing its way up and over the fieldstone wall.

All manner of things were emerging from all the rifts now. Not only creatures, but also colors, strange stones and even the smell of the sea. Then...a very familiar black leather boot stepped out of the original portal.

Gabriel!

Everything about him came rushing back to Julian. Gabriel's dirty mien, his slimy ways, his constant, pressing evil agenda. Was there no escaping him? Julian did the only thing his racing heart told him to do. He ran.

Out on the street, Julian found complete chaos. People scattered in confusion. Women screamed. Men screamed. Julian spotted a couple trying to cross the street, but this was no ordinary couple. This was a pair of

Neanderthals! Two cars driven by understandably shocked drivers collided in the intersection only inches away from the hairy, confused-looking cave dwellers.

Passersby floundered in a growing panic. Julian joined them briefly when…WHAP – an apple bounced off his head. Julian turned to see a cherub plucking apples from a nearby tree and lobbing them into the crowd – and that wasn't all.

Dozens of Egyptian slaves, roped together, tried to cut their bindings on the metal edge of a street sign.

Then he heard it. Despite the din, the pandemonium, Julian heard the sound he'd come to dread, a sound he couldn't seem to escape - no matter what!

Thump, drag.

His heart and mind racing, Julian ran past peacocks, a Renaissance-era clown, a group of Spanish Conquistadors and an unidentifiable six-legged creature that looked particularly hungry. Julian ran and ran, past zebras, kings, and a very lost Michaelangelo.

"Ragazzo! Ragazzo! Dove sono io?" Columbus begged of Julian, as he raced away.

Thump, drag.

Julian ran faster into the thickness of chaos, except now something compelled him to actually shut his eyes, trusting in his legs to take him where he needed to go. He only wished he knew where that was.

The thump, drag became like a tick-tock. Systematic. Methodical. Relentless. Resounding in Julian's very bones.

His legs on fire, his lungs burning, Julian stopped and bent over, his breathing ragged. "What am I going to do? How do I stop this..." He looked around at the hordes of screaming tourists and bewildered locals, "...this nightmare?" Then Julian took a shuddering breath and looked up.

He was now standing directly in the shadow of one of the biggest clocks in the world.

THIRTY-ONE

Boy vs. Man

Julian stared at Big Ben as if hypnotized. Terrified tourists swarmed around him, jostling him this way and that, but he felt as if he was frozen on that spot and the clock's mechanism was vibrating his body with every beat.

Finally, he inched closer to the tower, feeling every gear of the clock, every swing of the pendulum pulling him forward against his will.

Thump, drag.

Hysterical tour groups rushed madly down the spiraling steps of the tower of Big Ben. Julian was stunned when he saw what they were running from: a huge flock of shadow birds, just like the ones he had seen in the cellar! The claws of these otherworldly birds scraped the heads and backs of the terrified tourists as they ran, willy-nilly, for shelter.

Then, for no sane reason he could fathom, Julian began climbing the tower stairs. His body made him do it, as it marched him in a sort of clock-like fashion, while his mind argued, *No, no, no!*

Like a salmon swimming upstream, Julian waded through the fleeing tourists and now began to race up the tower steps, faster and faster.

He reached the top of the stairs then looked behind him at the dizzying stripe of red paint that traced the spiraling steps downward. A giant millipede, a thousand times normal size, was rippling its way down the stairs, bent on freedom. Julian shivered but continued to go up the stairs.

He didn't know where he was going or why, but he did know – he just realized – that he had business to take care of.

He pushed his way past Big Ben's great bell and then paused to consider something. Despite having lived in Westminster his entire life and having heard the bell toll each and every day, Julian had never seen the cavernous bell up close.

And what a sight it was, Julian thought: a symbol of majesty and power. To look up inside of it into the darkness of its crown was like staring through a portal into another world. But Julian didn't have time for sightseeing. He raced toward the observatory deck, grasping the iron guardrail for support.

The entire city of London was spread out before him. Just then a sharp wind blew Julian's hair from his face. Screams filled the air as frightened tourists leapt from the London Bridge into the water while others hung precariously from the towering Millennium Wheel, which had ground to an abrupt stop as a fleet of tiny alien spaceships circled it curiously.

Julian stared, aghast at the chaos all around him. It was as if the entire universe and every possible parallel universe had all arrived in London at once.

Suddenly the noise faded away into a stony silence. Julian heard only one thing.

Thump, drag.

"Alone at last." Again that voice! It came from a remote corner of the observation deck. Gabriel stepped out of the shadows and squinted his colorless eyes in the uncharacteristically bright sun.

All color drained from Julian's face as he caught sight of Gabriel.

"Please, don't let my handsome face frighten you." A deep laceration had claimed the left side of Gabriel's face.

Thump, drag.

Gabriel inched closer to Julian, forcing the boy to take a step back. A dance they'd done before.

Too many times, Julian thought.

The sky darkened ominously but Julian didn't have time to find out why. He was completely backed up against the guardrail. He had nowhere else to go.

"Careful. Don't want to fall," Gabriel said sincerely.

"Leave me alone!" Julian shouted shakily.

Gabriel stepped closer. Julian could smell his foul breath.

Suddenly, Julian did the unthinkable. He swung one leg, then the other, over the rail and onto the ledge outside the famous clock face.

The sky darkened deeper. Gabriel squinted up at the sun delightedly. "A solar eclipse!" *How perfect for me*, Gabriel thought, and followed the boy out onto the ledge while the sky continued to welcome his eyes into a cooler embrace.

Julian backed up and wobbled slightly as he looked down. An Assyrian Army was marching across the plaza below. A woman was screaming from the back window of a taxi. A giant anaconda had wrapped itself tightly around the vehicle. Nothing seemed to make sense.

Gabriel had come closer. Julian looked down. Nowhere to go. Then he looked at one of the mighty iron hands of Big Ben. It was the only thing left to grab, the only way to put distance between himself and this relentless madman.

Emboldened by the increasing chaos below and the blackening sun above, an idea struck a very delighted Gabriel. “I do hope you will forgive me, but I must try a little experiment.”

Julian didn’t like the sound of that. “What experiment?”

Too late for questions. Gabriel suddenly stepped forward and kicked away a chunk of wooden ledge beneath Julian’s feet, causing him to hang all of his weight from his grip on the hour hand of the clock. “Nooo!”

Gabriel watched patiently as Julian hung on for dear life. Finally the weight of the boy’s body pulled the hour hand down from the four o’clock position to the five, sliding Julian down further in the process.

But that’s not all that happened. At the very same moment, all that Gabriel had hoped for and more occurred. There was a monumental shift that both of them could feel deep inside their hearts.

Gabriel knew right away what had happened and, thus, searched for his reflection in the pearly white face of the clock. He watched as the fresh wounds on his warped face scarred over. The forwarding of time had healed them!

He smiled from ear to ear. "So it is true, after all. You are the Sacred Object."

Julian desperately struggled to maintain his grip. *What? Who is he talking to?*

That's when Julian noticed his own reflection. But what he saw wasn't his own face, exactly. It was an older version of him. Slightly more...mature. Front teeth that no longer seemed too large for his mouth. A jaw that was now slightly fuller. He didn't understand what was happening. What was Gabriel talking about?

"Don't you get it, boy?" Gabriel explained. "YOU moved time. Right now, everywhere – men, women, babies, pets, even insects are feeling something that only you and I can understand."

Julian shook his head no, but his body felt it was true. He could even feel that across town, on the floor of Chronus Family Cleaners, a new wrinkle had carved its way into Freemont's old face and his broken heart had begun to mend.

The sky grew darker yet as the citizens below looked upon their own sudden physical changes with shock.

On the clock tower, however, Gabriel practically giggled with delight. Almost gently, reverently, he looked at Julian. "Amazing. You have the ability to control time, Julian."

Julian's legs swung wildly, as his grip slipped on the hour hand putting him another inch closer to a plunging death. "No. It can't be."

"It is. You are indeed the Sacred Object."

Julian felt sick. *He* was the Sacred Object? What did that mean? What did any of this mean? And why did his heart hurt when the thought of Granddad skipped across his mind like a pebble atop a pond?

Gabriel could hardly contain his excitement, "Do it again, boy. Warp time again. Don't you see? You have the power of the universe in your hands! Do it again."

Julian's mind raced. Do what again? The things Gabriel was saying didn't make sense. They couldn't possibly be true.

"It is in your blood, Julian. Passed down to you by the father you never knew...my very own brother, Allister."

Brother? This sudden influx of information made Julian dizzy. Or maybe it was the shift in time, or the sun that had all but disappeared in the sky. Whatever the cause, Julian felt his grip on the clock hand slipping even further. His hands trembled with effort, his every muscle felt on fire.

Suddenly a flash of memories began to fit together like puzzle pieces: The way he had always understood clock gears without studying them. The way he felt them pulsing steadily in his blood. The games he'd played as a young child, pretending he could stop or speed up time. He thought it was make-believe. That it was all make-believe.

But...no. This was very, very real. Julian realized it as he gazed down at his dangling feet and the sheer drop below him. So much was now becoming clear. *Julian* was the one controlling time in Delphisola, not Granddad's antique cane!

It was *Julian's* panic that had forced the sinking quickstone to quicken outside the forest and *his* calm that made it reverse. It was *he* who had made the echoes of the past bounce back from the shallow cave and he, again, who froze Gabriel's scouts in mid-air.

In a flood of relief and dread, Julian realized that what his horrible uncle - His uncle! - had said was true... *Julian was the Sacred Object.*

Gabriel allowed his terrified nephew a moment to accept his fate. "We are family, Julian. And together we can do powerful things. If only you could see what I've seen in my travels. That pathetic dimension, Delphisola, is but a measly speck of filth on the cosmos. There are an infinite many more that await us." Gabriel extended a hand toward Julian. "Take my hand, nephew. Let us change our destinies together. Let us rewrite history. Let us rule creatures that make these pterodactyls look like kittens. We can go anywhere and anywhen."

Stubbornly, Julian held tight to the hour hand of Big Ben. "I've seen the effect you have on worlds, *Dark One*." Desperately, Julian looked for somewhere else to step, anywhere.

"We could even find your parents, Julian."

When Gabriel spoke those last words, Julian's breath was sucked out of him. He felt empty and sick. "They're dead."

Gabriel smiled indulgently. "No, they are not. And I'm willing to bet Freemont never told you they were, either."

Julian shook his head in disbelief.

"I'm sure he always chose his words carefully," Gabriel said, "As a careful man like him often does. My guess is he told you they were...*gone*."

Julian was becoming enraged. He would not allow this man to suggest his beloved granddad was a liar.

"Search your heart, Julian," Gabriel added.

Julian suddenly remembered every sentence Granddad had ever uttered about his parents. Every conversation about them had ended the same way, "*They are gone, forever.*"

There was no more time for games. There was no more time for denials. Julian turned to Gabriel and, for the very first time, met his eyes directly. "I'm listening."

Gabriel smiled and continued, "They were forced by an explosion into an alternate dimension, just as I was. The only difference is that their rift left no portal. But with your power and my talents – we can find their dimension and give you back the family you have always deserved. Never again shall anyone call you *orphan.*"

Julian's eyes welled up with tears. His parents. He could see his parents again. He could make them proud. He could feel their arms around him and hear their loving voices.

"I can teach you to control it, Julian," Gabriel's words interrupted Julian's momentary reverie.

The sky entered its final phase of darkness as the sun disappeared, now totally eclipsed. The screams and sounds of chaos below intensified. Torches were lit, if only to illuminate the nightmarish scene occurring: that of many dimensions converging into one. *Spillage*, as Bishop would say.

Overcome with a new confidence, one he couldn't identify, Julian swung his weight from the clock hand enabling him to leap across the broken ledge until landing on solid footing, face-to-face with his despicable uncle. "There's only one problem. Time is not for man to control," he said.

At precisely that moment, the bell of Big Ben began to toll loudly. The tower shuddered under its weight and sound.

Shaken by the sound, Gabriel stumbled then fell forcefully against the guardrail, collapsing it. Gabriel was now dangling precariously, his feet swinging wildly.

Gabriel looked around in a panic, unsure of what to do in this space between life and death, when his nephew's hand appeared in front of him. Without hesitation, he grabbed hold of it.

And in the moment that Julian and Gabriel were connected, they were electrified by each other's energy. The air around them grew heavy, time felt frozen, and all became silent. The chaos, the honking horns, it all disappeared. London was but a still photograph beneath them.

Julian struggled to hold the weight of Gabriel's wildly swinging body, which he had grasped as firmly as he could. Gabriel looked up at him slyly and grinned. "All you need to do is let go, Julian, and like your parents I, too, will be gone…forever."

Julian thought about it. Why shouldn't he let this man die? They would call him a hero for it. Everyone would.

Just then, the sky lightened, ever so slightly, although everything else remained frozen in time. The eclipse was ending. The sun would return very soon.

Julian looked down at the face of the pathetic, filthy Gabriel and smiled. *No.* That wasn't the way. With a sudden strength he could not explain, Julian pulled his bewildered uncle up to safety.

Gabriel smiled gratefully. "Clearly, you're a better man than I," he conceded. Then, with just the slightest nudge, Gabriel pushed his nephew over the ridge to his death.

THIRTY-TWO

Julian's Time

As Julian fell from three hundred plus feet, the sensation of endlessly dropping made his heart slow oddly, then skip. *This is it*, Julian thought. But then, as he continued to fall, Julian swore he felt Granddad's heart slow and skip a beat, as well.

What he didn't know was that, at that very moment, in the Keeper's Chamber, Freemont arose, suddenly strong and determined. "Julian!"

Julian's descent seemed to last an eternity. In some strange way, it was peaceful and beautiful. He saw the sun restore itself completely and beam its great ball of light over the tip of Big Ben like the beacon of some heavenly lighthouse.

Despite the way it was ending, Julian was at peace now. He knew he had done the right thing. He readied himself to hit the street when...

POOF!

Warm folds of soft darkness suddenly enveloped his body. *Is this it?* he wondered. *Is this what death feels like?*

Several moments went by before Julian realized he was not dead. No, he was very much alive and wrapped inside a seemingly invisible blanket of air and space, which folded around the way he once saw demonstrated by...

"Welcome home, lad," Bishop's voice called down as he uncovered Julian from the invisible fabric.

The light of day reappeared and Julian stood at the base of Big Ben. He was welcomed back by the familiar faces of Bishop, Sir Alfred and, wait a tick...Detective Riley?

Bishop pulled Julian up and hugged him for the very first time. And Julian was perfectly happy to hug him back.

Sir Alfred breathed a sigh of relief and shared an embrace with Julian as well.

Julian smiled once he realized that he didn't die, but his relief soon faltered. The streets were still filled with chaos. A tiny dinosaur the size of a chicken scurried through their feet and chased poor Petey off into the bedlam. And what of Gabriel?

Julian looked back to the top of the clock tower. Gabriel was nowhere to be seen. Julian knew that soon Gabriel would find the Black Taxi and escape yet again. But that was a problem for another time. "Sir Alfred! Bishop! We have to get to the clock shop, now!"

Julian hardened his look at the two old men. "I said *now*!" Julian took off back through the crowd. The two old men exchanged confused glances and then followed him.

Outside the AM/PM Emporium, a blockade of military vehicles had formed. Behind their protective cover crouched Colonel Chadwick Burroughs of the Royal British Brigade, and nearly one hundred soldiers at his beck and call.

Hunkered down with assault rifles drawn and pointed at the front door of Freemont's little clock shop, they seethed in anger as they listened to the sounds of their city crumbling around them.

The door to the shop stared back at them, left a few inches ajar from the last creature, a baby dragon, that had stumbled out of the fractured rifts in the cellar and mixed into their world.

Detective Riley determinedly pushed and bumped his way through the throng of soldiers until he reached the front of the barricade.

Colonel Burroughs was standing next to an army tank with its main gun pointed directly ahead at the shop. It was quite a war machine: the British Challenger.

"Colonel Burroughs! Colonel Burroughs!" Detective Riley called out.

The Colonel turned and took in Riley with a look of disdain. "Oh, thank goodness you've arrived, Detective. We can all rest easy now."

"Colonel, I present to you to Mr. Bishop Eberlee and Sir Alfred Taggart."

The Colonel spit his gum at their feet. "Nice to meet you. Now get the bloody hell out of my way."

Detective Riley insisted, "They can help you. They are men of science and history..."

Colonel Burroughs scoffed, "I have men of action, Detective. That's all I need. A group of soldiers ready to act on my plan when I command them."

"And what exactly is your plan?" Detective Riley pressed.

The Colonel inserted a fresh stick of gum into his mouth, chewed it several times, and then spit it out, hitting Bishop in the chest, who wiped it away indignantly. The Colonel summoned one of his troops. "Officer Collister!"

"Yes, sir?"

"Inform this nosey civilian detective what my plan is."

Officer Collister squared around on his heels and recited loudly, "To kill and capture any and all alien creatures that come out that door, Sir!"

Detective Riley, Sir Alfred and Bishop were speechless. *That is his plan?*

But then a fourth voice suddenly spoke for them all. "If that's your plan, then you don't have enough bullets," firmly declared Julian Rigby.

He nodded to Bishop and Sir Alfred and smiled proudly as he pushed his way through the crowd to stand before the war-hungry Colonel. "I live in that clock shop, Colonel, and I'm going home now."

Sir Alfred and Bishop's eyes never left the Colonel's.

The Colonel was stupefied. "What is this kid, an idiot?"

Without fear or reservation, Julian walked calmly past the Challenger tank and through the barricade of soldiers as he approached the open stretch of cobblestone in front of the shop.

The Colonel turned to his right-hand man, "Collister, toss that boy into the river immediately."

Officer Collister hung his head, not wanting to answer. He ignored the command in hopes it would go away.

Colonel Burroughs insisted, “Well?”

Officer Collister reluctantly set down his weapon and stepped forward to go after Julian, but Bishop immediately picked up the officer’s gun and drew it on the Colonel. “Anyone touches the boy, and the Colonel gets it. You all report to me now.”

Petey ran up and squeaked proudly on Bishop’s shoulder. Bishop translated, “And to Petey.”

From every angle, soldiers drew arms and shouted commands at Bishop.

“Withdraw your weapon!”

“Release the Colonel at once!”

“Give us the order, Colonel. We have a clean shot!”

Julian continued to walk calmly toward the front door of the shop, ignoring the chaos and panic swirling all around him.

The standoff was interrupted by the Colonel himself, who instructed, “Let the boy go inside. If he wants to die…that’s his problem now.”

Bishop held his aim steady so that Julian was free to enter the clock shop.

There was something about Julian’s demeanor as he walked confidently into the eye of the storm that Sir Alfred couldn’t help but admire. It didn't seem foolhardy. It seemed strangely heroic.

Softly, Julian gripped the same door handle he had turned so many times before. He suddenly remembered the first time he had come home from Westminster Under School and opened that door to find Granddad in his fuzzy sweater. He suddenly realized how much the clock shop had been a part of his life, and how it felt like home. Everyone watched in awe as Julian entered the clock shop, leaving the door defiantly open behind him.

Inside, Julian carefully stilled the pendulums of so many clocks that seemed to shiver with nervousness. Then, he set his sights on the open staircase to the cellar where light flickered from all the new rifts down below.

Taking a deep breath, Julian picked up his Rigby Coat-of-Arms clock and, once again, held it like a shield before him as he stepped down into the stairwell.

One slow and cautious step at a time, Julian descended into the source of London's chaos. He felt no need, this time, to pull the strings of every light bulb above him.

When he reached the final step, Julian stood firmly and gazed again upon the twelve rifts, laid out in a straight line like numbers of a clock that had unraveled itself. Julian couldn't even see the shape of the family heirloom anymore. Shifting prisms of light and a weird glow hid his grandfather's grandfather clock.

The rifts seemed to sense Julian's presence. They seemed to bounce about with nervous anticipation, like crazed fans at a rock concert as their hero took the stage.

With his shield in his left hand, Julian extended his right arm toward the twelve dancing rifts, like a shepherd to his flock. Suddenly, the rifts swelled even more! Julian could feel that they were pulling at him, as if they were yearning for his touch.

Somehow, Julian knew exactly what to do next.

He aimed his palm at the rift farthest to his right. Immediately, it was drawn like a bolt of electricity to a metal rod, funneling all of itself, all light and sound, straight into Julian's hand.

The influx of energy jolted Julian's heart.

Dust began to kick up and whirl at his feet. Slowly, Julian angled his palm to beckon the next rift, which also joined the first in channeling its energy into his hand.

The spark he felt inside magnified two-fold and gave him a supercharge of adrenaline like he'd never felt before.

Stepping slightly to his side, Julian moved his palm toward the third, then the fourth rifts.

Again, the forces surged and joined the others, compounding the electric feeling inside his body.

The humming sound of the rifts then rose in pitch, rattling the fieldstone walls of the clock shop. Small cracks appeared in the mortar between the stones.

Deep in concentration, Julian skipped past the middle rift, whose bright light completely concealed the family heirloom behind it. He summoned all the rifts to its left. Each answered the call of their master obediently. Each added its own degree of power and energy to the mixture.

Julian now stood amidst a whirlwind of dust and light - his left hand holding firmly onto his shield; his right outstretched to absorb the powerful currents of the eleven rifts that now vibrated, entranced, before him. *It is time to finish this*, Julian thought.

What he didn't know was that he had an audience. Sir Alfred had crept down the stairs behind him and was watching with awe and pride.

Julian shifted his palm once more to summon the original rift straight ahead. With a force as powerful as all others combined, it united with the others, nearly knocking Julian off his feet.

The light magnified a hundred times and so did the humming vibration. But, for the first time in his life, Julian did not falter. He felt no fear at all. He did not want to look to someone else for help. He did not want to run away. No, he knew that it was time for him to fulfill his destiny.

Somehow, he knew exactly what to say.

Dearest children of time and space,
Do not judge my boyish face.
I am your Shepherd and with your grace,
Will send you back to your rightful place.

Suddenly, a centaur came bounding down the cellar stairs from nowhere and ran straight past a crouching Sir Alfred and into the glow of the rifts, disappearing before Julian. Julian heard screams and gunshots as mayhem swelled outside.

He heard Bishop order, "Tell them to hold their fire!"

And the Colonel, still under Bishop's arrest, answered, "Hold your fire!"

The centaur was followed by the Aptaleons, the Neanderthals, the little dinosaurs and flocks of shadow birds, and then every other lost creature that had spilled from every other dimension into London. Pixies, harpies, cavemen, Picasso, Catherine the Great, dodo birds, they all funneled back into the radiant rift in a fast-motion parade of light and sound. Then, much to Julian's surprise, the officer that once mimicked his voice during his arrest in the clock shop was spit back out from the rift, his torso now stretched like toffee. Panicked and confused, the bobby scrambled up the stairs, screaming like a baby.

Then one last creature fluttered down into the cellar. It was the Mourning Dove that had followed Julian home from school and cooed outside his window.

Julian smiled at the bird. "I was waiting for you, little dove. And I know someone else who is, too. Back inside you go."

The Mourning Dove then vanished in the light.

Julian readied his stance once more. He slowly brought the Rigby Coat-of-Arms clock shield toward his chest until it interrupted the flow of energy, and deflected it all back into the original rift of the family heirloom in an explosion of light and sound so loud that Julian thought he would never hear again.

The rift that Granddad had kept hidden for so long was now sealed...and gone forever.

Outside the clock shop, shattered glass was everywhere. The Colonel and his mighty squad picked themselves up off the ground, recovering from the power of the blast.

Bishop rushed into the shop, trying to make his way down the cellar stairs through all the dust and debris. "Julian, my boy! Sir Alfred!" He squinted and coughed. "Julian? Tell me you are still alive!"

There was no answer, only silence. Bishop coughed again as dust swirled around him. Looking around wildly, he called again, "Julian!"

Suddenly, Bishop heard another cough – not his own. From his crouched position, Julian arose, still holding his clock shield in one hand like a mighty warrior of time. He stood tall with the eyes of a man who now knew exactly who he was.

Sir Alfred grabbed Bishop's arm and pulled him downward, where, on bended knee, they both saluted the powerful figure standing before them. "Keeper, my Keeper," Sir Alfred recited.

"Keeper, my Keeper," Bishop repeated.

Julian turned. He could not have been more pleased to see them. "Does this mean I can join your Bridge Club now?"

The two old men could not contain their joy.

THIRTY-THREE

Changing of the Guard

The Mourning Dove whirled and twirled through the wormhole, thoroughly confused by the colors, lights and sounds that washed over it. Sometimes spinning right side up, sometimes upside down.

Finally, the poor bird emerged into a completely dark landscape.

The bird's delicate wings, still brushed with the pulsating silver light of the wormhole, soon began to flutter, and, the landscape of Delphisola began to come alive.

A wave of light and color swept along the surface of the sluggish, oily lake, transforming it into a crystal blue sea. Dolphins began to arc and dance along its foamy waves.

In the Enchanted Forest, the barren Willows blossomed with greenery as thick as fluffy blankets. The bushes once hidden in darkness were now alive with lush ruby and violet berries, and the cocoons that had trapped so many creatures in the branches of the trees suddenly burst open with a tidal wave of brightly-colored butterflies that flitted this way and that in the fresh, new air.

The Mourning Dove flew past little Wilfred; still plunging in a free fall after being knocked away from Eleazar by Gabriel's scout – but right before the little caterpillar reached the ground something incredible began to happen to him...something he had been waiting for all his life. His metamorphosis!

Finally, he transformed into the most beautiful butterfly of them all.

Side by side, Wilfred flew with the Mourning Dove over his beloved land with a lump in his little throat and pride in his little heart.

Delphisola's three purple crescent moons suddenly sparkled like crystals, then faded away to finally allow the return of three suns that orbited a fourth many times their size.

These suns revealed a glorious golden orange and pink sunrise rivaling any sunrise in any world, and it was the first sunrise that Eleazar was ever able to watch.

He stepped with wonder from out of the Enchanted Forest. His mouth fell open and two words fell gently from his lips, "The Savior." Eleazar turned to the ten thousand fairies watching the magical sunrise along with him and shouted with joy, "The Savior!"

The Mourning Dove then flew over the surface of the Ponderous Pond, which began to glitter and move beneath the warm rays of the many suns. The lily pads bobbed peacefully, their little clocks once again ticking as dragonflies swept gracefully over them.

The dove soared over the deep crack in the soil where Pythia's granite pedestal had once stood. Slowly, the crack closed, sealing itself like a wound healing with time.

Then the dove flew directly into the dark fog, transforming it instantly into a fluffy white cloud that rose higher and higher until it touched the ceiling of the sky, again watching protectively over all citizens of their world.

The black crystal desert suddenly bloomed with life and a rippling waterfall appeared in an oasis. Near the oasis, a very perturbed ladybug, now completely covered in countless age spots, rolled her long-lashed eyes in disbelief. Could it be? Could daylight have finally come to Delphisola? Was time moving forward again?

The Mourning Dove alighted on a branch heavy with fragrant peaches, and rested.

Nearby, on another branch, the black crow that Julian had come to know, peered inquisitively at the dove.

With an almost imperceptible nod between them, the two birds simultaneously took flight. As they soared higher and higher, circling each other, the crow slowly changed color from black to white. The two partners then flew away together, wings beating in unison.

Delphisola had now completed its transformation. The air was once again fragrant, birds were once again singing, and the warm suns once again drenched all with a soft, golden light. Spring had returned to the island paradise.

Back in London, in the Keepers' Chamber, another change was taking place.

As Lily and Martin watched solemnly, Freemont beamed at his grandson with enormous pride. "Julian Allister Rigby, firstborn of my firstborn, you and your friends have shown more than your share of courage these past few days and have earned your place among the Society, not just as members, but as Elders." Freemont then turned the wheels of his brand new wheelchair carefully to face Bishop, Sir Alfred and Linus. "The Keepers' Bible, please."

The three gentlemen immediately obliged as they carefully handed Julian, then Lily, then

Martin a thick leather-bound book with gold-embossed pages.

Freemont spoke again, “Each of you, take a knee and promise to protect time from any and all those who threaten it - now and forever.”

Julian fell to one knee and bowed his head over his Keepers’ Bible, but then he glanced up and smiled at someone very familiar.

It was the fire hydrant.

Detective Riley smiled back at Julian, and then gave him a friendly wink. They were on the same team now. “Now that you’ve saved the world, Julian, what’s next?” Detective Riley asked with a grin.

Julian thought for a long moment, and then answered calmly, “Next? Westminster Academy.”

The chamber erupted with laughter and applause.

Lily and Martin, however, weren’t so impressed. “Seriously, Jules?” Martin whispered.

Lily added, “Yeah, where’s the adventure in that?”

Julian held his smile for his small audience and tried his best to whisper to his friends through his teeth. “Nah, mates. Not seriously. Next...we find my mum and dad.”

Acknowledgements

Special thanks to my wife, Angela, for not only enduring my obsessions - but for actually encouraging them.

To my editor, Julie Gray, who first suggested that I had it in me to write this novel and who so expertly guided me through each step of the journey.

And to Dee-Dee, for making books such a part of my childhood and for giving this one a most careful eye.

14681404R00198

Made in the USA
Lexington, KY
13 April 2012